Peirene

KAMAL BEN HAMEDA

TRANSLATED FROM THE
FRENCH BY ADRIANA HUNTER

La compagnie des Tripolitaines

AUTHOR

Kamal Ben Hameda was born in Tripoli in 1954. In his early twenties he moved to France. He now lives in Holland, where he works as a jazz musician and writer. Kamal has published several collections of poetry. In 2012 *La compagnie des Tripolitaines* (*Under the Tripoli Sky*) was nominated for a number of prizes, including Le Prix Ulysse and Le Prix du livre Lorientales.

TRANSLATOR

Adriana Hunter has translated over fifty books from the French, including works by Agnès Desarthe, Véronique Ovaldé and Hervé Le Tellier. For Peirene, she has already translated *Beside the Sea* by Véronique Olmi (Peirene No. 1), for which she won the 2011 Scott Moncrieff Prize. Adriana has been shortlisted twice for the Independent Foreign Fiction Prize.

MEIKE ZIERVOGEL
PEIRENE PRESS

This is a fascinating portrait of a closed society. On the surface this quiet vignette of a story could be read as gently nostalgic, but underneath the author reveals the seething tensions of a traditional city coming to terms with our modern world. The book gives us privileged access to a place where men and women live apart and have never learnt to respect each other.

First published in Great Britain in 2014 by
Peirene Press Ltd
17 Cheverton Road
London N19 3BB
www.peirenepress.com

First published under the original French language title
La compagnie des Tripolitaines
Éditions Elyzad, 2011
Copyright © Kamal Ben Hameda, 2011
This translation © Adriana Hunter, 2014

ISBN 978-1-908670-16-8

Designed by Sacha Davison Lunt
Photographic image by James Sparshatt /
Axiom Photographic Agency / Getty Images
Typeset by Tetragon, London
Printed and bound by T J International, Padstow, Cornwall

This project has been funded with support from
the European Commission. This publication reflects
the views only of the author, and the Commission
cannot be held responsible for any use which may
be made of the information contained therein.

KAMAL BEN HAMEDA

TRANSLATED FROM THE FRENCH
BY ADRIANA HUNTER

Peirene

Under the Tripoli Sky

I dedicate this book to the wives and mothers who,
for years, have demonstrated once a week outside
the state department buildings in Benghazi,
Libya, asking for the bodies of their husbands
and children who lost their lives on the night of
25 June 1969; women whose searing loss has gradually,
imperceptibly, reignited the flames of dignity.

True natives of this region were savage, hairy, toothless barbarians whose rutting season never came to an end, so they mated constantly, like their neighbours the monkeys. They gave birth to many mutant monsters and left them to die, gorged on by the local fly population.

Homo sapiens *from other continents called this country the Sea of Monsters, a place inhabited by cannibals, Cyclops, pygmies and hermaphrodites.*

The land was surrounded by steep cliffs and impenetrable mountains. Animals, imprisoned in their solitude, roamed here alone or in herds. The ground seethed with giant black snakes which fed on ostriches and antelope. These snakes left nothing for our ancestors, who never bothered to follow the reptile's track, for it devoured everything.

In those days the barbarians hunted fierce wild beasts and gentle gazelles. Their tribes lived in caves and they buried their dead – or what was left of them after an onslaught by our nation of flies – under a tumulus of stones or a dolmen.

They admired birds, feared the sun and venerated snakes, which were constantly reborn before their very eyes. They depicted snakes with the sun disc above their heads and flanked by two feathers to represent sacred wings. They wore lion tails and monkey tails, and at night they decorated themselves with rams' horns to assert their virility.

Their women were warriors and hunters by day, vaginas and wombs by night.

The priestess Maboula warned them that the sea was bad-tempered and unpredictable; she forbade them to go near it. She prophesied that a people who worshipped gold and gems would come to subjugate them if they ignored her instructions.

The men took care of the children and were heartily bored, so they ventured closer and closer to the coast.

And one day her vision became reality.

Sails appeared on the water's curved horizon. The boats drew on to the beach and men from the north sprang ashore with gleaming weapons. They appropriated the land and set up camp, watched from afar by the clutch of savages with deep dark eyes. Every time the invaders set sail they left behind all sorts of delicacies and drinks, particularly wine and beer; and the savages tasted these liquors, suspiciously at first, but soon they were enslaved. They were prepared to do anything to experience such pleasures again, forgetting Maboula's prophecy. And they made contact with the Phoenician sailors, who eventually set up drinks stalls all along the shore.

The barbarians accepted the most lowly tasks and became bearers and serfs in exchange for wine and silphium, the aromatic medicinal plant with magical powers to nourish the body, drive out disease, wash away weariness and soothe the soul. They no longer listened to any of Maboula's warnings, and the invaders called upon their princess, Dido, to scratch out the priestess's eyes to rob her of her prophetic visions once and for all. But before slicing off her head with her own nails, the defeated priestess put one final, terrifying curse on the laughing savages: 'You will be damned until the end of time. Other men will come to humiliate and enslave you. You will only ever be slaves and the sons of criminals.' Then she turned to Princess Dido and added, 'You will end up like me: abandoned, a pitiful object of contempt.'

Dido had not considered the consequences of her act. The reckless drunken men took all the power for themselves, deaf to the pleas of their women, who by now were merely bellies into which they emptied their desires. When subjected to these same laws, Dido burned herself on a pyre to escape forced marriage.

Ever since, there has been an endless procession of death, destruction and invasion in the land, much to the delight of the Free Nation of the Flies.

—EXTRACT FROM *The Book of Flies*,
ANONYMOUS

The day before.

Everyone already knew about it, except for me.

When I saw Aunt Fatima at the door I instinctively understood that a plan was being hatched.

That night she came to my bed to tell me her usual goodnight story:

> *Seven girls inside a flute. The ghoul twirls and*
> *twirls and eats one of the girls.*
> *Six girls inside a flute. The ghoul twirls and twirls*
> *and eats one of the girls.*
> *Five girls inside a flute. The ghoul twirls and*
> *twirls and eats one of the girls.*
> *Four girls inside a flute. The ghoul twirls and*
> *twirls and eats one of the girls.*
> *Three girls inside a flute. The ghoul twirls and*
> *twirls and…*

I always ended up falling into her arms, soothed and bewitched.

*

Aunt Fatima was the only person who told me the story
of the twirling ghoul that keeps coming back to the house
where the seven girls live. She was a widow and spent most
of her time with her only child, Houda, whose every whim
she tolerated. 'Big fat Houda!' the local children taunted.
I too would tease the girl as I ran away from her through
the long, narrow alleyways of the Medina while she tried
to keep up with me under the scorching midday sun. I
would hear her behind me, breathing heavily, dragging
her feet, and sometimes she groaned and sometimes she
wailed. Then I would stop and wait for her and want to
make up by stealing a kiss. But she always ducked aside
in horror, afraid she'd fall pregnant!

Aunt Fatima and Houda would visit for all sorts of
family ceremonies. And every year they arrived with the
first new moon, heralding the beginning of the fateful
period of fasting.

'Tomorrow there will be a celebration, your celebration!'
Aunt Fatima promised me as she chewed noisily on her
acacia gum softened with wax. '*Seven girls inside a flute.
The ghoul twirls and twirls and eats one of the girls. Six
girls inside a flute. The ghoul twirls and twirls…*'

'But, Aunt Fatima… are there really only seven of them?'

'Hadachinou!'

'But…'

'Go to sleep, little one, go to sleep!'

*

Daybreak.

The last vestiges of sleep were still weighing heavily on my eyelids when the naked light of dawn slowly appeared, spreading across the carpet. I stretched and closed my eyes again to preserve the image for a moment, but the first rays of sunlight danced over my face as if to thwart me and snatch me from my voluptuous indolence.

Deep inside the house, no one.

I walked through the rooms filled with silence and a thousand motes of dust rising in sunbeams, spiralling steadily in apparent chaos towards a secret, absent centre. I went over to a mirror and prodded my body, running my fingers over my forehead and the outline of my face.

Out of defiance I opened the shutters to look at the sun, eye to eye. Through the cool blue of daybreak and the multicoloured phosphenes skittering around me, I took a deep breath of crisp morning air and stretched again, an alley cat beneath a freshly lit sky.

Light spilt over the house and the walls and the corridor and the kitchen... which is where I went in the hope of finding something to bury the sense of exile that was beginning to overwhelm me. I gobbled a piece of fruitcake, then hurtled down the stairs like a punctured balloon. The magic of waking had given way to a feeling of powerlessness.

Nothing.

I sat on the doorstep and checked everything was real out in the street. I saw distant figures appearing in a hazy morning torpor – my mother's friends, who gazed at me tenderly and smiled.

'Time, there's nothing but time!' exclaimed a passer-by.

Before my eyes – now robbed of their fickle dreams – the tarmac and the ever-present sunlight.

On our terrace, Ibrahim the local butcher stood facing a bleating orphan lamb. My father always trusted him to select the victim when he came on his annual round for Eid al-Adha, the Feast of the Sacrifice.

But it wasn't Eid today!

Each year, the same gestures performed with perfect skill. The same fascination on children's faces... all the way to grilling the head and the feet.

The sheep's squalling, on and on, right up to the last moment, right up until its head is under the knife, when it sees the gleaming blade... It stops, accepts, gives up and watches its own decapitation with already glassy eyes. Blood spilling.

The sheep left to empty itself of its blood. Taboo food. Sacrilege.

Witches, jinns, the godless and the mad drink animal blood to revive their strength. But my mother gave it back to the earth with a shudder of fear and disgust.

I witnessed the ceremony with a mixture of amazement, curiosity and quasi-morbid delight. The sheep's silence, its eyes changing colour, its furious bleating as it faced the deafening void, the children standing round in a circle holding their breath, and the springing fountain of blood.

Ibrahim's sharp knife cutting smoothly through the skin as he whistled a well-known pop song.

Rivulets of slow-flowing blood, smaller streams coagulating.

The carcass left to the women: removing the offal, the intestines, cutting up the meat, salting it and hanging it out in the sun on the terrace.

The slow, impatient morning quivering.

Images of what was happening, what happened each year in this millennial ancestral ritual, spooled through my mind like an age-old dream brooded over again and again.

Noon.

Head lowered, I walked in and out through the front door, waiting for something to happen.

Hunks of the lamb hanging over the sink. Bones piled up like a still life.

My mother already at her pots and pans, preparing celebratory dishes, baking *assida*: wheat flour, olive oil, date syrup.

I went over to her with half-closed eyes.

'We're going to get you dressed and shave your head,' she said with a twinkle in her eye. 'Today's the big day.'

*

Dressed in only a simple length of white cotton cloth dotted with patches of saffron and wound round and round me to cover my body, I myself wander round aimlessly.

The deserted street; my yellow ball bouncing, bouncing, and the sun sitting in the sky, static and jealous.

I stand still and my gaze follows those two orbs abandoned in space.

The horizon squints, disinterested.

Tired, I let go.

In front of the mirror I stared at my new hairdo: the 'barber' had used his well-sharpened knife to shave my scalp from my left ear to my right with the help of a round metal plate, leaving one small lock of hair at the front.

My big head looked like a yellowing melon with a tuft of maize fibre. A sad scarecrow or – in the words of one of the women who had started appearing, all beaming smiles and brightly coloured *tistmal* headgear and the snap of acacia gum between their dazzling white teeth – like someone who'd just woken up.

Intrigued by the amused expression on all these women's faces and delighted with the sudden attention, I showed them my ball.

And the sun still incandescent in an impassive sky.

A group of men arrived at the corner of the street, friends of my father's. Eyes to the ground, one behind the other, they walked towards me as I sat on the doorstep. They stepped over me without a word or a smile and climbed up the steps.

I followed them, mesmerized, desperate to know what was going on.

In the hallway my father greeted them with hand-shakes and directed them ceremoniously towards the living room.

They sat in a circle on *mindars*, large comfortable cushions stuffed with wool. Every now and then a sharp cough betrayed a longing to smoke, or a voice would mutter a 'Bismillah!'

A hand rapped on the kitchen door; this was the signal.

My father stood up, left the room and returned with dishes laden with food.

The men ate, some of them avidly, others with more restraint, tackling the stuffed sheep's stomach, the grilled liver, the testicles, which were a delicacy, and other less noble cuts.

My father served red China tea and grilled peanuts.

The sun continued blasting the room with light, and all at once I became the centre of attention.

I proudly threw the ball against the wall and caught it again, showing off to this group of silent, cross-legged men.

They peered at each other for a while… then joined collectively to say, 'In the name of Allah, the Entirely Merciful, the Creator, Owner, Sustainer of the Worlds.

You alone do we worship and You alone do we seek for help. Guide us to the Straight Path. The path of those whom Your blessings are upon…'

The barber who had shaved my head finished intoning the Sura Al-Fatiha, the first Sura of the Qur'an, holding his hands up with his palms open to the ceiling.

A heavy silence followed.

He asked me to step forward.

Trusting as I am, I don't even think of taking refuge in my usual place, the terrace outside. I already know I can no longer escape the coming ordeal.

I don't close my eyes. I gaze up at the ceiling and picture the glassy look in the sheep's eyes on the day of sacrifice, a look full of renunciation.

The barber takes a razor blade in one hand and my foreskin in the other, and prepares to cut it. Only now, at last, do I gauge the extent of the threat and try to get away; two men leap up and hold me firmly.

Blood springs out.

I lower my eyelids to protect myself and, for the first time, delve deep inside myself to find the place where I can safely watch episodes of my life, like someone sitting at a window and watching the never-ending entertainment of the street through the slats of a shutter.

*

Lost in this indefinable chasm, I suddenly became aware of an explosion of women's laughter from the kitchen, a burst of cheerful voices lilting with the sheer joy of life and jostling together like a mass of balloons released to mark a feast day. What the men were up to was clearly of no concern to them. Meanwhile, the men filed past and put banknotes under my cushion, then slipped out, leaving a silence punctuated by my sobs and those of my two brothers, who had suffered the same fate as me.

In the still of late afternoon the women continued to busy themselves. They prepared couscous with onions and chickpeas, flavoured with cinnamon and orange blossom water.

In the back bedroom, my brothers stopped snivelling, gazing powerless at the low ceiling. I wailed to the point of exhaustion until, caught out by the smell of cinnamon, the dancing shadows and lights, and a brief silence, I fell asleep, succumbing to the improvisations of time.

Indistinct figures hover on the far side of the door.

'Good morning!'

I don't answer.

My mother, Aunt Fatima and Houda in their night-dresses, standing one behind the other.

'So,' they persist, 'our little man's growing up! How are things with your little bird?'

A moment's hesitation. Then they just can't help themselves and burst out laughing. The three of them leaning against each other, my mother and my aunt holding their breasts that jiggle as they laugh, while Houda has crossed her arms over her great shaking tummy.

I didn't say a word.

'Never happy. Did you see his face! Looks like an grumpy old owl!' my mother concluded as she closed the door again.

Nothing.

I slipped out of bed and found my 'little bird' wasn't hurting, so I went downstairs, melted into the walls and very gently... flew away!

Scatterings of laughter continued to pierce the dawn silence.

I escaped. And for three days I loitered outside in the streets, wandered across wasteland, skulked in the alleyways of the Medina and walked along the seafront to the old port. Here I watched the fishermen gathering in the morning to drink their red tea brewed in terracotta pots over coal fires in *kanoun* burners. And here I watched them meeting again in the evening to empty whole crates of beer, while they ate broad beans and chickpeas and grilled sardines.

Tired of grumbling my way round my secret hideaways, I eventually decided to return home. Aunt Fatima and Houda had gone back to the country. There was no one left to tell me stories before I fell asleep.

Seven girls inside a flute. The ghoul twirls and twirls and eats one of the girls...

'I can see you on the terrace, sitting there like a zombie on the marabout's tomb. Just look at you! Here, come and help me make the tomato purée.'

My mother was bustling about in every direction; she had lots to do before her guests arrived for the tea ceremony after the siesta. She often received visitors, but today there was a strange glint in her eye. What mystery meeting did she have planned?

'Hadachinou, you crush the tomatoes with your feet while I take care of the meal.'

Standing there in my basin of tomatoes, I was already smacking my lips in anticipation. *Richeta!* Hmm-mm! Delicious noodles cooked in spicy tomato sauce, swimming with broad beans, haricot beans, chickpeas, fennel and sun-dried mutton, all heightened with the sharp edge of a drizzle of lemon. My mother made the noodles herself. She did it all, all by herself: preparing *ilghidid*, the sun-dried meat, doing the laundry by hand, kneading the bread dough, which I then took to the public ovens, and tending the chickens and vegetables. She never stopped, except for her siesta and when she had guests.

Like today.

She packed me off outside. I had finished crushing the tomatoes and had emptied them into large earthenware jars, so she sent me off to deliver a package to Aunt Zohra next door. '… And then stop off with Aunt Hiba to do her shopping, and also see if Fella needs you at all – her daughter might be with the Americans today. And you can see if…'

She could always find a valid reason to get me out of the way.

When my mother gave me a package for Aunt Zohra I always knew what was in it: tea or coffee, and fruitcake. Because, to her great shame, Zohra's husband, Uncle Abdou, left her with nothing in the house to offer visiting relatives. Even though he ran a grocer's shop. His fruit and vegetables were never very fresh, and he really couldn't have cared less: he owned two small houses, which he let out to two families, Mr Bosanca's and Mr Garibaldi's, the local baker. Meanwhile he, Abdou, sat outside his tiny shop, keeping the coal fire going under his *kanoun*, where he would boil up the same brew of tea for the umpteenth time.

Sometimes I pinched some fruit from him and took it back to Aunt Zohra, who hid it, quaking with fear, to give to her two daughters, puny, mewling creatures like a couple of starving kittens. My hand still bears the mark of one of my marauding exploits. One day, when I snitched a beautiful bunch of grapes from him, he caught me at it and ran after me, shrieking, 'Come here, little devil, give me back my grapes!' Terrified, I lurched through our half-open front door, but in my panic I closed the door on my own hand. Uncle Abdou, though, was careful not to come and complain to my father, whose penetrating stare filled him with dread.

It was painful for me taking those bundles to Aunt Zohra. Not that I didn't like her or that I was afraid of her husband. He sometimes even proved kind towards me. He would sit outside his shop and keep me beside him to tell me stories about the old Tripoli, back in the day.

'Hadachinou, did you know that during the Italian colonization, the Tripolitans used to boil up dates – yes, dates – to make tea?' he would ask me yet again as he offered me a drink that I politely declined. The grown-ups drank tea or coffee, sometimes with a piece of baklava or some other sweetmeat, but what I liked was *gazouza*, the local lemonade. Uncle Abdou was far too tight-fisted to give me that.

It was Zohra's shyness, her awkwardness, that bothered me. Her embarrassment rubbed off on me, and I ended up paralysed and unable to speak. When I arrived at her house she would know why I was there and she'd come over to me, hand outstretched but unable to look me in the eye. Then she'd just stand there, eyes lowered, silent and motionless. If she did manage to open her mouth it was always to say the same thing: 'Hadachinou, next time you come I'll give you a sweet. I haven't any left today.' And her head rolled slowly from right to left, and left to right, very slowly, like in a slow-motion sequence in a movie.

That morning I didn't wait for Aunt Zohra to open her door. I left the package on the doorstep and ran off as fast as I could to avoid that same hangdog expression and the same empty promise: 'Next time you come...'

It wasn't much fun seeing Aunt Hiba either. She too backed away from people in shame, even from me. She didn't want to show her broken teeth or her face with its fresh bruises from the latest blows inflicted by her husband, Uncle Saïd, who went through life with a big full belly, chain-smoking and raining down blows and instructions on the unfortunate woman. He beat her whatever state he was in, drunk or first thing in the morning, and on any grounds. Not enough salt in the couscous or, no, too much! She'd overdone the flavouring or, no, she hadn't put in enough!

How much turmeric should she add to avoid marital strife? Aunt Hiba would hurry over to my mother for help measuring out the exact amount of turmeric to flavour her dish of rice and onions, and satisfy her husband's fickle taste buds. She was always frantic when she arrived, a look of panic in her eyes like someone who's been bitten by a rabid dog and can feel themselves gradually succumbing to the disease without even the hope of release from an instant death. She suffered from high blood pressure and diabetes too. 'Serves you right,' her husband shouted. 'If you didn't keep stuffing your face with all those platefuls of food...'

He used to invite his friends over once a week to get drunk: all men together eating, drinking and exchanging local stories through the night. Aunt Hiba prepared the finger-food for them, she had to think of everything, it all had to be perfect: peanuts, grilled almonds, little mutton sausages fried till they were just right, cheese, spicy green olives and black olives in aromatic herbs, salted chickpeas and broad beans, hard-boiled eggs, anchovies and, to round things off, *imbakbaka*, noodles cooked in hot, spicy tomato sauce, which was to disperse the reek of alcohol before the guests left with the first rays of the sun. And even if they were all well fed and happy, he still sometimes hit Hiba: she'd looked at him disrespectfully – in the eye!

I had a shock when I went up to see Aunt Hiba to do her shopping that morning.

I climbed the stairs to their house on the rue Miquel Angelo. The front door was open and I suddenly heard screaming. Aunt Hiba was wailing like a camel being slaughtered for the Feast of the Sacrifice, a poor creature dying in public ignored by passers-by. Frightened, I crept towards the sound. The bedroom door was ajar. Aunt Hiba was quite naked, wearing just her slippers on her feet, and Uncle Saïd hit her, hit her again, then pushed her roughly. She fell on all fours. His penis was straining towards her, a huge erection like a mule's, and he took her.

Ever since that day I felt guilty and was overcome with shame whenever I had to go and see her. And, without realizing it, she picked up on my discomfort and would say, 'Go on, thanks for your help. Go and play. You mustn't stay here with me. Just a boring woman who still doesn't know how much turmeric to put in her husband's rice after all these years. Your mother went to all that trouble for nothing... I'm useless, a pointless, boring aunt. And I don't have any stories to tell you or money to give you for sweeties. But I've got some biscuits here, if you want. I made them for your uncle's tea this afternoon.'

I preferred going to see Fella, who also lived on rue Miquel Angelo. There I recovered my lost exuberance. I was her chosen one, the one who carried her basket when we went shopping together and her valiant knight when I set off on my bicycle to find a great hunk of ice for her. I would bring the ice back in her big jute bag under the scorching sun and unbearable heat of summer, and when the *ghibli* was blowing in August and September, when sand from the desert swept through Tripoli, and no one went out unless they absolutely had to.

Fella really loved honey sweets, particularly the ones flavoured with rose water. She often cooked them herself on an old stove in her tiny kitchenette, using a slow flame to simmer the caramel made of pure spring water, acacia honey, lavender and rose water. Then she generously offered it to everyone in the neighbourhood. So I knew that whenever I dropped in to see her there would be plenty for me to get my teeth into. I would savour it with her daughter, Touna, who was only young but already worked as a cleaner for the Americans on the Mallaha military base near Tripoli.

Fella very occasionally went to the synagogue in the Harat al-Yahoud, the Jewish quarter deep inside the Medina looking out over the Mediterranean. It was a beautiful building, but it's long since gone. She sometimes took me with her, and it wasn't like going to the mosque with my father, which was boring, and where I wasn't allowed to speak or move. The synagogue was completely different: I could do what I liked, and people ate and drank. I actually think Fella only ever took me there on feast days. She liked having fun and telling stories. Touna, her poor sullen daughter, often felt abandoned.

When I got to Fella's house that day she wasn't there. Touna told me to wait for her, that she'd be happy to see me and needed me to do some shopping for her at Tonino's grocery. Touna offered me a glass of orangeade, which I savoured slowly. She looked at me sadly. Except when she was working, she was always on her own. She didn't go to school, didn't have a father, and Fella didn't earn very much in her job as a seamstress. The local Italian women were fierce competition, particularly Signora Filomena, who single-handedly met the needs of almost all the Muslim households in the area. My mother knew how to sew but sometimes left difficult jobs to Fella, not that this ruffled our neighbour Signora Filomena's feathers. So Touna had to do housework in soldiers' homes, and that didn't bring in much money either. From time to time she would come back with soap or tea... She was poor and, to make things worse, people thought her ugly.

I personally didn't see her as particularly unattractive, but she'd been told it so many times that she ended up believing it and kept herself more and more shut away.

'I'm ugly,' she said. 'No one believes I'm her daughter. Even you, you don't come to see me   she's the one you come to see. You feel you have to stay here with me, but do you think that makes me happy?... No one likes me...' And she dissolved into tears.

'No, Touna, no! That's not true! I play with everyone. Why would you say that to me, Touna? I don't understand. I like seeing you. It's more like you're the one who runs and hides as soon as anyone appears.'

Oh, what could I do to cheer her up? It has to be said, her mother was always off in her own little world, a world of games and silences, or the wonderful world of madness she conjured up when she got carried away telling her stories. She had her own way of telling them, perfectly aware of how much I revelled in listening to her bewitching voice. At times it was as if even Touna no longer existed. Then Fella would break off guiltily: 'You're my darling, Touna, you know that! I loved you before you were even born. I knew you before you came into the world, when I made you with your father, under a fig tree overlooking the Mediterranean.'

Touna wasn't the first person I'd heard saying, 'Nobody loves me.' Signora Filomena got there first. My mother and I went to her house one afternoon and found her collapsed in a heap on the carpet in the living room. She was crying, 'Nobody loves me. I'm tired and you, all of you, you couldn't give a damn!'

I stood rooted to the spot, but my mother listened patiently.

'Don't worry, Signora Filomena, everything's going to be fine, and I've got a remedy for your stomach ache: an infusion of thyme... You need to drink a lot of it with honey, but you'll see.'

'I'm frightened, Signora Aziza, I'm frightened. What if I have to end my days somewhere else? I'd die so far from Tripoli. My husband keeps saying we'll be driven out of here one day.'

'Don't be frightened, Signora Filomena. I'll be here to defend you... And, anyway, why would anyone drive you away? Who would do you any harm? You were born here, you're Tripolitan, you're locals. You eat Tripolitan food, you speak Tripolitan, you dream in Tripolitan. Don't you worry, I'm here.'

Signora Filomena's family had been in Tripoli for three generations. She and her husband, Mr Bosanca, had three daughters, whom I enjoyed playing with, Maria, Flora and… I don't remember the third one's name, the one who wasn't so keen on playing with me. On summer evenings they would grill sardines in their small garden next door to ours. They stayed out late, drinking rosé and chatting. I used to watch them through the shutters; spurred on by the wine, Mr Bosanca would try to woo his wife, but Signora Filomena often hung back.

'I'm worthless, nobody loves me…' Signora Filomena wailed that afternoon.

'No, Signora Filomena, that's not true,' my mother repeated. 'It's not your fault, it's because of the war. You're my neighbour and my friend.'

But there was no calming her. She gripped her stomach and wept in pain. My mother knew what was causing her pain, and so did I for that matter. They spoke in veiled terms in front of me but I knew… The moment I moved away I heard Signora Filomena confiding her secrets to my mother.

'Yes, my grandfather used to do that to me when he looked after me while my parents were away. Yes, my grandfather, Colonel Fabio.'

Signora Filomena wasn't always so gloomy. When we all went to Place d'Alger to eat ice creams or pizza, her daughters and I knew how to draw the occasional smile from her. Or was that down to the beer she drank in glasses clouded with condensation?

When she offered to take me somewhere with her daughters my mother was the picture of gratitude, but I didn't accept these invitations without a moment's unspoken hesitation: would I have to go to that dark church on the square in order to earn my ice cream? The Signora sometimes made me go there while she carried out her devotions, and it was so boring! Those priests, furtive in their black robes, the solemn folds of their ornately stitched surplices swishing over the marble floor and the endless tide of litanies reverberating into the very depths of my stomach. I waited impatiently for the Signora's last genuflexion. Then it was pleasure time!

Signora Filomena would take us to the pizzeria, where each of us could salivate over his or her choice of either a pizza with tomatoes and oregano-flavoured anchovies, or an ice-cream with a subtle vanilla taste set off by crunchy slivers of bitter chocolate. She herself preferred the bar opposite and its famous sandwiches: grilled sardines between two slices of crusty bread whose dough was impregnated with olive oil infused with garlic and red chillies.

Afterwards the five of us – four ladies and one little gentleman – would go for a walk in the park, stopping to sit and rest on the grass, gazing at the Mediterranean and letting the sound of the waves gradually win us over.

When she was relaxed like this, lying on the grass while her daughters played a little way away, Signora Filomena talked to me about my great-aunt Nafissa, whom she adored, and she always asked for news of her. Aunt

Nafissa and Signora Filomena had become friends the moment they met at my mother's house. Now whenever my great-aunt visited from Djerba, she made a point of seeing the Signora: the two of them sat for hours drinking wine and holding hands. My great-aunt Nafissa understood her troubles.

'Your grandfather's no different from the rest of them. Apart from their bellies and their pricks, the only thing men are interested in is destroying with one hand what they've just created with the other. I remember the war, the famine and the way women were raped when the Italian soldiers entered Tripoli: they spread shame and loathing through the city. After the Greeks, the Romans, the Vandals, the Arab tribes and the Turks, it was their turn to try out their virility on our bodies. And they're still at it now, they're just wearing different clothes. Sewer rats, the lot of them. They swagger about in front of their wives and children, but when they get together in their bistros and their mosques they draw in their horns. They're deceitful and servile when they don't have any power, and depraved and offensive when they do.'

That was the sort of thing Nafissa said. My great-aunt Nafissa. I loved the woman too, what a character!

She liked to sit on a rug in the sunlight, outside the house or on the terrace, chain-smoking and telling us about her past.

'I've spent my life in Djerba, that really was the life! I captured plenty of hearts there. You wait till you grow up, my little Hadachinou. But then one day a beautiful man managed to capture my heart, and that was when I knew what real love was. I couldn't sleep, couldn't eat, couldn't think about anything but him; I was possessed. But he didn't love me, he didn't want me. I was already a smoker then, and in the evenings I used to go down to the beach with the Jewish and French women, and we'd stand with our feet in the Mediterranean drinking *boukha* or that delicious palm wine called *laghbi*. At the time I was devastated by the dismissive way he treated me, but I'm relieved now. If I'd married him I would have lost my freedom. He was a very devout Muslim. You'll know what I mean when you're older. And there it is. Since then everyone's avoided me, looked down on me; they say I'm an easy woman. Even your family, my family, keep their distance, saying they're ashamed. I want to go back to my Djerba. The people here in Tripoli are too hard; they don't understand anything about love.'

And she saw that love was the root of Signora Filomena's troubles.

'You see, Signora Filomena's god is love… and I mean pure Love. That's the problem. Anyone who doesn't know hate will never know love, and the things we don't want to see, the things we hide and keep locked away inside for too long, will get out sooner or later, they'll explode. Feelings are clouds and we can't do anything to stop the clouds. Do you understand, my little angel?'

I lied a bit to Aunt Nafissa, acting innocent and saying I didn't really understand anything about love between a man and a woman, but I knew it could be tragic, like with Zaïneb.

'Ah, Zaïneb,' she sighed, her face dropping. 'She was young and beautiful and so intelligent! Such a shame! She was free, like me. But I ran away when they wanted to marry me off. I didn't want anything to do with that man. Zaïneb couldn't, poor thing. The things they make us put up with on this lowly earth!'

Zaïneb used to come early in the mornings to take me shopping for vegetables in the Medina souk; my mother had no more freedom to go out than my aunts. The only people in the souk were men and young girls who were yet to be married. The only women you saw there were Jews and Catholics.

Zaïneb and I had a lot of fun racing up and down the flights of steps on the street, carrying on until we were exhausted. She read me children's stories, tales from the *Thousand and One Nights*. Sometimes she would sing songs by the Egyptian singer Oum Kalthoum, or Andalusian love songs. She had a rare quality: a lust for life. Then all of a sudden she stopped coming. I couldn't believe it, but my mother told me she wasn't allowed out any more; she would soon be married to an important man. I immediately thought of Josef and felt sure Zaïneb would be very happy, so I started laughing with glee, but my mother glowered at me, her expression unreadable, and walked away.

Josef was a local young man whom Zaïneb waved to surreptitiously when I was with her, perhaps to test my loyalty and discretion. And what was bound to happen happened: coming back from our shopping trip one day she said, 'By the way, we're going for a picnic in the Gazelle Gardens tomorrow and I'll introduce you to a man who's not like all the rest.'

I flushed scarlet with jealousy and rage. A man! Not like the rest! Fat chance! And, as if she'd anticipated my response, she added gently, 'I'll have to get married sooner or later, you know. It's better if I choose my husband myself, otherwise I'll die of a broken heart... Don't worry, you'll always be my friend. In fact I've told him all about you because he's seen us together. I told him that if we got married I'd still want to see my Hadachinou.'

The next day I set out with her under Tripoli's imperturbably blue sky. I walked with my head lowered, more out of shyness than jealousy. Josef was already there by the gate to the gardens. At first the only thing I noticed about him were huge dark eyes and full red lips... smiling. He and Zaïneb held hands in silence and I followed along behind, head still down. The next thing I knew they were sitting on the grass, and so was I, but some way away. They held each other's hands gently, sitting there in that little park, which was often deserted. They didn't speak but looked into each other's eyes and blushed, while I watched and felt increasingly disappointed and resentful: they were behaving as if I just wasn't there. They'd only brought me along to avoid prying eyes, so that we looked like a nice little family sitting peacefully on the grass, enjoying the sea air. They were lost in each other's gaze. But for me that afternoon went on for ever.

'I've got to go,' Zaïneb said suddenly, moving away from her boyfriend. 'There's someone over there who knows me. If he tells my family he's seen us together, it would be a disaster. You'd never be able to ask to marry me then. Come on, Hadachinou, quickly,' she added, dragging me with her.

I remember their wistful gazes. He put his hand discreetly over his heart and she responded with the same gesture as we backed away.

She headed off through the streets, hardly thinking what she was doing, and I tugged at her dress and reached for her hand, peering up at her as if to say, 'You've forgotten all about me!'

A smile stole across her lips, then she laughed out loud and started running, ignoring men who turned and stared in amazement at this shameless young woman tearing past with me trotting along behind.

As everyone knows, the things we wish for and the things that actually happen rarely tread the same path. The man who was to be her respected husband was not the man of her dreams, but someone I'd never met. Neither had she, for that matter. For some obscure reason, my mother then forbade me from seeing her, but, being a stubborn child, or perhaps responding to an inexplicable impulse, I stole off to visit her at siesta time. The sun was blazing mercilessly that afternoon and, as I drew closer through the torpor of sleeping streets, I heard screams slicing through the silence like a punishment or a curse. In the distance I saw a shrieking, tottering figure, a living torch: to escape her marriage, Zaïneb had set herself alight with petrol.

'Anyway, what was I saying? Oh yes, marriage! It's appalling,' Aunt Nafissa continued, 'churning out poor bloody girls who'll be slaves all their lives and boys who'll keep them at the grindstone and weave a web of boredom to the death. No. Really, no!'

'Not all women can do what you did, Aunt Nafissa,' my mother replied flatly, adopting the submissive indifference she showed to all senior members of the family.

My mother never wanted to tell me about her marriage. 'Later, another time, when you're older. I can tell you about my childhood, about the famine and the Italians colonizing the country. Do you know, at your age I was already an apprentice. I used to go to the craft market, and do you know what I did? I embroidered rugs. My father was a sandal maker and wanted me to learn a craft. He took me out of the Italian school the day they packed all the children off to greet Mussolini when he arrived in Tripoli. Your grandfather wasn't having that, but I think he actually needed a good excuse to make me leave school. I had to work – we didn't have enough money to live on, and your grandmother Halima had to stay at home because she had so much to do. Some women would go out to work in other people's houses, but your grandfather was far too proud. I wanted to stay at school and study, to become an engineer or a teacher in a girls' school. I would have earned a living, and I wouldn't have been dependent on whatever my father spared me to buy the bare essentials. But there was no money left at all in those days; people were short of everything, even drinking water. I remember one year when we were *so* hungry! I lost all my hair… I had such lovely hair, right down to here – longer even, down to my knees. I was very pretty, and before your father came and took me, I used to walk proudly through the streets of Tripoli and all the men used to look at me. No one looks at me now. I've grown huge and ugly. I'm fed up with this house, this street, this whole city. Sometimes I pray to Allah that the last day will finally come, that the eternal fires will consume us all. I was a beautiful flower but the sap's been sucked out of me, and now all I'm good for is to be thrown on to the rubbish heap. I've turned into a monster like the ones you go and see at Luna Park, at the fair…'

When I was alone with my mother she often went over these lamentations again and again, the same litany every time… 'I was a gazelle, people couldn't take their eyes off me. When I fell pregnant with you my skin started to wrinkle, my face puffed up and my legs got fatter. Since having you I've tried to get back my looks and my energy. I've changed for ever. I'm ugly now. A monkey, I'd say, or worse, a fairground freak… Just look at me! My skin all stretched, and look at these rolls of fat, this great stomach that I can't even hide under my clothes,' she would say, horrified at herself. And she would rant on and on, not taking any notice of me.

I thought my mother was beautiful and I couldn't understand what she was talking about. Fairground freak? OK, she'd always been a bit cuddly, but why did she loathe her body so much? I could show you some real monsters…

At the end of spring every year the Tripoli fair took place. This was an event I looked forward to with curiosity and impatience. I spent all my free time there and stored up my adventures so that I could come home proudly and reveal them to my astounded mother. The exhibitors used to hand out free brochures – on every subject, including advertising for agricultural machinery – and I had fun collecting them. Then, at the end of the day, I would dot these splashes of colour over a green lawn in a park or bring them home in the hope that my mother would take me seriously when she saw me reading like a big boy. She often grumbled, not very impressed with the latest technological advances… and this evidence of my pseudo-knowledge would end up in the bin.

I always saved up the fun of going to Luna Park until late on Friday afternoon, the weekly day of rest in Tripoli. That way I could combine all my pleasures in one go, because Friday was also when we had *bazine*, a very special dish of dromedary meat with tomato sauce and polenta, a meal you eat with your hands, sitting on the ground around a large platter.

There were rides at Luna Park, of course, and plenty of other attractions, lots of games and stalls stretching away as far as the eye could see. But I didn't have very much money, just enough to buy some sugar-coated grilled peanuts, which I dipped into sparingly; or enough to visit a couple of attractions, but no more. So I went to see the freaks, the human monsters.

Their tent was in the middle of the site. At the door stood a tiny man, shorter even than I was, a dwarf, exhibiting a great slumped mass of flaccid human flesh beside him.

'Come and see the monsters! The Seven Wonders of the World are nothing by comparison, not the Pharaohs' pyramids, not Machu Picchu... Roll up! These fantastical sights have come here to your city of sand and dust. Come and see with your own eyes things you will never have seen before... Trust me, you'll get your money's worth. Roll up! Come and see the girl covered in fingers and the bearded lady, the snake-man and the face-lady! Come on, fight your way in...'

That name, 'face-lady'... I was intrigued. I wanted to go in just for her. The cashier, a toothless little old woman, looked me up and down, and down and up, and I noticed that I was plunging my hands in and out of my pockets without even realizing it. At last, with my ticket deep inside the pocket, I set off down the labyrinthine corridor with its tented black walls. I walked slowly, breathlessly, so as not to make any noise, hugging the wall to make myself invisible and not disturb these counterfeit creatures. A hairy bearded women with an ugly mop of dark hair suddenly loomed into view as I turned a corner. Her piercing eyes pinned me to the spot; they had the same nasty, suspicious expression as the destructive, pillaging rats that terrorized our city. Poor woman, she just sat there quietly on her chair, knitting! I looked away and tiptoed off, eventually coming to another open space. And there she was, right in the middle: a woman's head with sad, distant eyes like the eyes of a sheep that knows you're going to slit its throat at daybreak. But then the face came to life and gave me a sideways glance. I was so surprised, I couldn't manage any reaction at all. I stood there in silence, turned to stone by her insistent stare... A smile started to hover at the corner of her lips.

'Good day, good day to you, little man. My name is Narcissus, like Narcissus in the myth. I'm just a face, just a gaze.'

I risked a smile myself.

'My name's—'

'Wait! Don't say a thing! I'm going to try to guess your name. No, actually, I'm going to *give* you a name. Would you like that? And it's going to be Ghostiman, will that do? I only give names to the ones I think are sweet and tactful. I saw how careful you were as you came in, so gentle, a friendly little ghost.'

'No, my name's not Ghostiman. It's—'

'Shush! You're a ghost wafting through my life like all the others. They often take the shape of nightmares, sometimes of dreams. If you want to be my friend and for me to love you, let me call you Ghostiman. Come back tomorrow. I'll tell the doorman to let you in. Tell him you're Ghostiman, faithful courtier to Narcissus, and whatever you do don't tell anyone about your visit here, not your mother or your father, because if you do I'll know. I want this to stay our secret. It would be best if you come at siesta time, when everyone here is having a rest. We don't open to the public till later. Give me a kiss. Yes, go on, on the mouth. Don't be shy. I won't gobble you up – I'm saving you for tomorrow.'

I skimmed a hasty kiss on her forehead, then fled. My whole body was shaking. Perhaps I'd committed a sin? I ran towards the exit and tore through the streets, not noticing anything on the way, not even the herd of dromedaries that a glowering Bedouin was driving through Tripoli, his furious shouts trailing after me for a long time without interrupting my flight.

I arrived home out of breath. My mother was in the kitchen and in a good mood, but as unconcerned as ever about my excitements. She was humming the refrain of an Oum Kalthoum song: '*Oh, let me lose the day when my heart did not taste love…*'

'Eat your egg! How was the fair? Did you have fun? Aren't you hungry? You usually eat like a horse. Go on, eat, otherwise I'll feed it to the cats.'

I loathed cats, but she could give them whatever she liked on that particular evening.

'What *is* the matter with you? Do you want a biscuit, or maybe some bread with tomatoes and olive oil?'

My mother didn't insist; she knew that, as and when I needed to, I would slip out of bed to ferret around in the kitchen for something to eat. But it was thirst that disturbed me more during the night. I fidgeted around in my crumpled sheets, breaking out in a cold sweat, with a great lump in my throat. I couldn't sleep: the moment I closed my eyes Narcissus's face and her delectable lips appeared, and that mouth whose kiss I hadn't felt able to accept, it fascinated me, as round and red as a cherry, sweet as baklava, fragrant as a peach. I struggled with feelings of terror and pleasure.

The next morning, probably to recover from my unusual lack of food the night before, I had a blowout, filling up on the delicious, sumptuous *richeta* my mother had cooked. With a bulging stomach and fired up by my plans, I told my mother I was off to take my siesta in the little room at the back, the coolest place in the house, which acted as a larder in those days when we had no fridge. Astonished by her offspring's latest hare-brained idea, my mother just raised her eyes to the heavens, slowly exhaling as she murmured the words 'Allah protect us!'

I lay down on the bag of wheat my father and I had taken to grind at Uncle Mousbah's mill for Friday's *bazine*. I waited for a while, holding my breath and straining my ears, then at last, when the clink of plates stopped and I was sure my mother had gone up to her room for her own siesta, I scampered down the stairs like a little field mouse, as fast as I could, my feet kicking so high that they smacked against my buttocks with every stride, running to be with her... with Narcissus.

At Luna Park the tarmac had grown tacky in the heat – despite my efforts to look after the shoes my grandfather had so lovingly made for me out of the best leather, they were now covered in tar. When I reached the big tent I was ashamed and ended up taking them off, hopping about to stop the soles of my feet being burned by the incandescent sand. The doorman appeared out of nowhere, took my hand and urged me to go in, then disappeared equally mysteriously.

Inside the tent, it was slightly cooler, but the sweat continued to spring from my every pore. Was it the excitement? To overcome my fear and avoid being jeered at, I launched myself into her room, pretending to be out of breath, ostentatiously wiping sweat from my brow with the palm of my hand and shaking my soaked shirt, which clung to my skin. Then, adopting a casual tone to disguise my shyness, I said, 'I'm sorry I'm late. I had to run... my mother asked me to help with the washing-up.'

Narcissus laughed at the sight of me.

'Take off your shirt. You'll find some towels over there to wipe yourself down. Take off your *saroual* and your underpants. Don't be frightened. I've seen boys with nothing on before.'

I flushed; my heart was beating like a cauldron about to bubble over.

'Go on,' Narcissus continued with a smile. 'Get undressed. Yes, that's right, you can cool off. Go and dip the towel in the basin. Yes, over there. Does that feel better? Come here, come to me. You haven't had a siesta and neither have I. I was waiting for you. We can have a siesta together if you like. Leave your clothes. You're not putting them back on yet. They won't take long to dry.'

Standing naked before Narcissus, I didn't dare move.

'Come on, we're going to have a siesta in my room on a real bed, and I'm going to tell you stories. Do you like listening to stories? You're shy. Don't be frightened. Take me to my room. We'll be comfortable in my bed, you'll see. That's right, there's nothing to be afraid of. Light that taper; the matchbox is right next to it. There, that smells nice, doesn't it? It smells of narcissi. Do you know this smell? It's very sweet, isn't it? Come here beside me, let yourself go... Take me in your arms, yes, like that. Would you stroke my hair?'

I closed my eyes and let myself drift through a world of dreams, abandoning myself to it. The light in Narcissus's kohl-edged eyes was reflected in the sheen of my skin. She the face-lady and I the mirror-body, we wandered through meandering subterranean galleries peopled with disembodied faces of men, women, boys and girls, and in my sleepy state their sadness reminded me of the black men I had seen along the walls of the Banca di Roma, shoeshine boys who smiled at me and seemed to have been waiting there for all eternity for something they knew didn't exist, but the very act of waiting for it gave it some legitimacy. Then Narcissus's empty, inward-looking eyes turned towards me and, barely moving her lips, she murmured, 'I'd like to introduce my little boyfriend…'

I didn't tell my mother or anyone else about that peculiar afternoon, and at siesta time the next day I ran off again; but when I arrived quivering by the door to the tent, the doorman stood in my way.

'What do you want, boy? It's not opening time yet.'

'But it's me, Ghostiman. I came at the same time yesterday. I was seeing Narcissus and you yourself—'

'Go on, off with you. Go home. There's no Narcissus or Ghostiman here. Go on, scram, or I'll never let you in again.'

Under a shameless, merciless sun, I trailed around like a lost Sloughi with nothing to relieve my boredom. So I set off in another direction and my feet took me down towards the sea, back to my usual refuge behind the rocks. I unbuttoned my short-sleeved shirt, folded it as I'd been taught to and laid it carefully by the water's edge. Then I stepped out into the Mediterranean. I stood smacking the waters of that calm peaceful sea, trying to stir up some waves and unleash a storm. Eventually I returned to land exhausted; the sea in its serenity, witness to so much despair, had defeated me. And soothed me. But the sun was still hanging insolently in the sky and, lured on by tiredness, I headed home to my street. The door downstairs was locked. I gave a few hesitant little knocks. No one. My mother was probably visiting one of her friends, drinking tea and chatting 'to pass the time more quickly', as she often said.

I went round to Signora Filomena to use the stairs which led up from her garden to the next floor and to our kitchen door, which was never locked. Signora Filomena offered me the ritual glass of chilled lemonade that I so loved, but the ready excuse of a migraine meant I could escape the obligatory conversation; I didn't feel like talking. I opened the kitchen door a crack and heard laughter punctuated by whisperings.

I stepped forward cautiously and saw them through half-open curtains, in the muted light of the living room. Wrapped in a single peaceful moment, like a beautiful calm sky after whirlwinds and storms, wind and rain have cleared. Simply there together: my mother and her soul sister, her alter ego, Jamila. Two innocent, well-behaved girls who wanted nothing else than to spend time together uninterrupted, their bodies resting full length on a humble old carpet and their arms dancing about to articulate their words more fully. I instinctively knew I wouldn't be welcome, so I went off towards the cemetery and sat down beside the tomb of marabout Sidi Mounaider, watching the sparrows scattering into the wild raspberry bushes.

Over the next few days I felt confused and baffled, no closer to understanding what had happened at Luna

Park. I told my story to no one, and if anyone asked why I was unusually silent – me, the child who never stopped asking questions, who hopped about like an inquisitive flea – I told them the truthful lie that I'd got sunstroke at the fair. After a couple of weeks my adventure had faded. I was me again, the boy who became invisible when the women shared their afternoon tea ceremony, happy to sit there listening to them talking about their Tripolitan lives and dreams. But my licentious experience must have kindled my curiosity, because I studied their kohl-lined eyes and the pink make-up that brought their full lips to life, and with their every move I inhaled the fragrances exuded by the gauzy fabrics they wore. I was more keen than ever to insinuate my way among them, even though my mother wanted to share this time alone with only her closest friends, such as Jamila, without the suggestion of a man's presence, not even a boy as 'sweet and innocent' as me. It was obvious to me that my mother secretly cursed the fact I was there, but didn't dare send me away in front of my grandmother Halima, or my great-aunt Nafissa, who would chew vehemently on her acacia gum as she leapt to my defence.

'Let him stay. He's only a boy.'

'Well, from the look on his face you wouldn't think so,' my mother replied. 'He's a crafty one, I tell you. I made him, so I know what's going on inside his head. He never plays with the other boys, you know. He's always on his own, and you'll never guess what he plays with. A doll, that's right, a doll! And I take it away from him every time, and he comes back with another one every time, as if he made them himself. And what for? He pulls off their arms and legs, gouges out their eyes, opens up their stomachs. I tell you, Auntie, he's debauchery in the making.'

The other women laughed at what she said, not bothered that I was in the room. My mother didn't insist, forgetting I was there as she attended to her duties as a good hostess: brewing tea, handing round biscuits and making sure everyone was comfortable.

But when Jamila, her childhood friend Jamila, visited she did everything she could to get rid of me. On these occasions my mother was jittery and was prepared to sacrifice her meagre savings to encourage me to disappear; she sometimes even gave me enough money for a cinema ticket, or she sent me off to my grandmother Halima, or came up with some errand that needed running immediately. When my mother started the day by singing '*On the banks of love, our boats came ashore, and we were united in passion, along with our friends…*' I knew the afternoon would be devoted to Jamila, for whom my mother always had time to spare.

Nothing outside.

Not even a light morning breeze. I'm sitting on the front doorstep and the usual beams of sunlight are streaming over the decrepit walls, delivering their sibylline messages in vain. I've forgotten how to read them.

A dancing figure appears in the distance, further up the street which is permeated by a desolate silence.

Jamila! It's Jamila!

Jamila reaches the house in an exuberant state, her rounded buttocks quivering beneath her gauzy kaftans, her fleshy lips half open as the acacia gum snaps loudly between her teeth, made-up like a Hollywood star right down to the insolent beauty spot drawn on her left cheek. She greets me with a conspiratorial wink.

'So, little man, you're still here,' she says, and her laugh explodes like shattered glass.

I stay where I am, a tousled figure, like a cockerel plucked of his tail feathers and left on the doorstep. As she walks through the doorway she stops for a moment to brush down the fabric veiling the curve of her hips, removing an imaginary speck of dust, then she goes inside without giving me another thought, carelessly knocking into me and glancing over her shoulder with a 'funny-looking thing!' She laughs and carries on energetically snapping her acacia gum.

The sound of footsteps rushing down the stairs. Smiles and kisses. I stand up and follow in her wake of jasmine and eau de cologne. When I find her I stop in my tracks, hovering to one side, gently nodding my head.

They send me outside – 'go and play with the other children!' – then forget about me and head off together, perhaps into the back bedroom on the terrace, or into the living room. I picture them as I've seen them before… lying on the carpet, propped up on cushions that sag as they gesticulate, their kaftans rising up as their legs slide furtively between each other.

They forget about me but I'm there, catching glimpses of them through the gaps where the tented awnings cross, watching.

There they both are, smiling as they gaze into each other's eyes, then laughing and laughing again. Their eyes, their whole bodies, say how happy they are to be together, lying on that carpet in their light clothes, just there, with no need for words, blessed by dancing light filaments bouncing off the walls of their refuge. The softened brilliance of late-afternoon sunbeams caresses their faces, two women restored to a childish, carefree state, transformed by the joy of being reunited.

*

Jamila stayed the night at the house. The next day was a feast day to celebrate the end of fasting, and she helped my mother bake baklava and other sweetmeats to be shared for the occasion. As for me, when she was around I couldn't sleep.

At daybreak, her supple, floating footsteps.

I crouch outside her bedroom silently. She's standing silhouetted against the open window and I can make out the sway of her hips as she switches her weight from one foot to the other. Her rounded buttocks protrude beneath her thin nightdress, cleaving together along the angle of her hips like twin apples hanging from a branch.

She's contemplating the still-virgin sky, sliding a hand over the oval of her face and cupping the palm of her other hand to hold the weight of her unsupported breasts. I feel the smile flickering over her face.

Outside a childish blue is entertaining the watchful sun as it rises and traces the contours of old houses on our deserted street and outlines Jamila's slender upper body, which is now leaning forward and stretching out to secure the shutters to the wall, leaving my astonished eyes to feast on only one thing: the flamboyant fullness of her womanly buttocks.

She turns around and walks towards me quickly.

'It's going to be hot today. I'm off to sprinkle water all over the house, then I'll close the windows and doors to keep it cool inside.'

Unaware that my gaze is lost in the dark undulations of her pubic hair, which keeps appearing through the transparent fabric of her nightdress, she steps agilely – and naively – over me. And I'm left sitting there naked, huddled over my childish distress, beside the now empty bedroom with its lingering fragrance of intimate smells and the eau de cologne she wears.

'Go on! Go and play outside instead of hanging about under my feet. Go on! Otherwise I'll tell your mother.' Then she gives me an absent smile and I…

When Jamila was there my mother rediscovered her lust for life, her childishness and the urge to speak.

She didn't speak to me much, but when I mentioned Jamila in a by-the-by tone intended to hide my all-consuming jealousy, her tongue was magically loosened.

'Jamila's more than a sister to me, she's my soul, my secret. We were born on the same street. We went to the Italian school together, then when Mussolini came and we had years of scarcity and abject poverty, we both lost our hair at the same time, and when it grew again we checked each other for lice, the only creatures that benefited from the situation. Her father was killed by the Fascists and her mother disappeared, and she was crazed with grief. My parents took her in. We both had to go and work on the looms in the craft market to earn a bit of money; we were barely twelve years old. Later your grandfather gave us away in marriage, but even then we stayed faithful to our childhood memories… Jamila's my sister, my heart, my mirror, my very own soul…'

I often followed them at a distance when they went out for walks incognito through the streets of the Medina, hidden from prying eyes beneath their traditional *four-rachïa*, which turned them into ghost figures like the rest of the women. On days reserved for women, they went to the *hammam*, or they visited the black sorceress Hadja Kimya for a talisman or an amulet. Sometimes they stopped to buy a coloured scarf called a *tistmal*, or a piece of fabric to make a new kaftan, and they went to the spice market for incense and acacia gum. I never managed to work out exactly what happened when they were with the sorceress but, sure enough, they always came back from there with a spring in their step and full of life. I can still hear them arriving home while I crouched in one of my hiding places.

'If he's happy in his mosque, he can stay there,' my mother said, laughing.

'And mine can get lost inside his bottles,' Jamila said, going one better, 'and you won't find me trying to save him. Let him enjoy it and let him drown in it!'

And they both collapsed, laughing noisily like a couple of schoolgirls delighted with their jokes, or perhaps just glad they could poke fun at things that made their day-to-day lives a misery.

My father, a solitary man given to prayer, shut himself away in the small bedroom at the back of the house when he came home from his shop or from the mosque. He was indifferent to the people around him, locked in his own world in the company of Allah. As for Uncle Hadi, he spent his nights in the company of other drunkards. 'If their young wives want some fun and relaxation, they have to search for it elsewhere,' Aunt Nafissa often commented, with her usual bitterness towards the male gender.

Sometimes during the tea ceremony, when my mother had slipped out briefly to stock up on the coal that was so essential for the *kanoun* or to put some finishing touch to the cooking, strange mutterings would circulate among the women, instantly becoming highly charged when some of those present – and it was always the same ones – made insinuating remarks about Aunt Jamila's secret life.

'She's never at home... She's so provocative to all the men when she goes shopping in the Medina... My neighbour's seen her going into the sheikh's house several times, when his wife's not there, of course, probably to beg him to speak to Allah on her behalf and ask him to give her a child... Apparently she's been seen around the American neighbourhood, she gets picked up in their cars to go...'

But my great-aunt Nafissa had heard all this gossip before, and if anyone so much as mentioned Jamila in her presence she would flush with rage.

'Leave Jamila alone,' she cried. 'Let her live her life. It's only because you're jealous that you see evil in everything. She and her friends allow themselves freedoms you don't have, freedoms you envy because your husbands keep you on a tight leash. What would you have her do? Stay at home like you, sitting on cushions and sucking on *loukoums* while you wait for men who never come home? You think those women are living bad lives? You make me laugh! But you don't know when to hold your tongues, that's for sure, and you're full of spite. And, anyway, it's not as if any of this has ever stopped you taking their money!' she added, always ready to speak out against injustice.

She was referring to a women's association that Jamila and my mother had established which allowed members to take it in turns to buy something they really needed or wanted. The fact was neither they nor any of the others had any money; all they had was what their husbands were prepared to give them for the bare essentials. By economizing carefully they had a little left over and this they pooled at the end of every month; thanks to their cooperative, each in turn had her chance to buy something that her own funds could never have allowed. Jamila and my mother mockingly called this their *Jamïya*, their benefits fund.

If they had 'behaved shamefully', as these treacherous wagging tongues implied, I would have been the first to know. I followed them like a shadow, all my senses on the alert. I tracked them like a hunting lion, but often ended up bored of this pointless surveillance, and would leave them to their regular circuit of innocent diversions if something in the street or the shady alleyways of the souk caught my attention.

Basically prostitutes, my mother and Aunt Jamila, judging by what was said behind their backs. And there

I was pursuing them and looking out for the slightest misdemeanour... Ridiculous!

I knew plenty of prostitutes, poor girls. I used to go and stand on their streets to watch the men coming and going outside their doors, during siesta time or as evening fell, when all the women had gone home for the day and I'd grown bored of chasing sparrows with a palm frond through the Sidi Mounaïder cemetery, or of sitting daydreaming on a freshly dug grave.

I cut through the Medina and arrived at the shady area, known for its dubious activities that the city shrugged off to its periphery, the fleapit cinemas, street vendors of every description, the black men who polished shoes on the dusty ground. Most of their customers were heading for the local brothel and had their shoes cleaned to while away the time until they were shown through those doors that admitted a queue of regulars one by one, men of every colour, from every corner of the land, all lined up in orderly fashion.

The first time I went there I was still a bit shy, hanging back slightly. But I was intrigued by the customers and revelled in the women's shrieking laughter and their acerbic quips.

I came back.

After a few days the prostitutes started noticing me.

My mouth hung open like a playful dog's, and I had no idea that the girls on the terrace of the brothel were stifling their laughter, pointing out my childish flabbergasted expression to each other. When one of them came down, took me by the hand and led me into that kingdom of half-naked bodies, I didn't put up any resistance.

Not many children lurked about in these places that bristled with various connoisseurs of fresh meat: English sailors on leave, dockworkers, Bedouins on a jaunt. They would tease me: 'Let's have a look at your little willy!' Then they'd invite me to share... the precious chocolates the sailors had given them. The kindest was Khadîdja – she filled me with a combination of confusion, admiration and fear. She had a handsome blue-green tattoo from the middle of her forehead down to her chin, her lips were the red of a fig split open to be greedily enjoyed, and her eyes – yes, she had eyes like a tigress about to pounce – sparkled in a thousand different colours. She was the most sought after, but she granted her time and favours to only a few men, having them sent straight in through a door reserved for regulars, among whom I was more than a little proud to be included.

When she winked at me from the brothel door, I was the chosen one; it meant she was free, that she could see me, often to talk to me or just to offer me a treat. Her voice became melodious. She talked about her childhood in the mountains, where she'd been free as the wind, tending to a small herd until her father sold her to a spice trader from Tripoli, not realizing what a pimp was – as far as she knew, anyway. I pretended to listen rather than actually hearing her. I was bewitched by this goddess of Tripoli, unable to take my eyes off her and hanging on her every word, as they say. Until one torrid summer's afternoon. Suddenly she broke off and wiped her brow with the back of her left hand.

'So, little man, you've stopped listening to me,' she whispered. 'You're like all the others, you're not listening. All you men ever listen to is your own bodies and what they want.' She snatched my arm – I was shaking by now – and drew me to her, rubbing herself against me.

'Is this what you want too?' she asked.

'No, no. *I* love you, I want to stay with you.'

'Go away,' she laughed. 'There's some baklava on the table. One of my customers brought it. Take as much as you like. Go and play outside. Don't worry, I'll still be here.'

Back on the street, feeling upset and humiliated, I walked with my head lowered, kicking a pebble, hounding it furiously like a grumpy child, a spurned male.

'I'm not listening, she says. Rubbish! I always listen to women. And if I don't listen to her properly, then it's her own fault. She'd better start telling me children's stories, and anyway, women should be the ones listening to men, that's the law,' I railed inwardly, resorting for justification to accepted practices that I usually loathed.

To be honest, I *didn't* pay much attention to what Khadîdja said, and perhaps that's why I lost touch with her. I was a child, primarily interested in self-discovery; quivering in response to forces that I didn't suspect but that she knew how to elicit, and therefore deaf to what she was confiding.

But with other women I could listen to them talk for hours on end, all of them. I listened to Fella, I listened to Nafissa and others who were less outspoken and whom I only vaguely remember; with them I felt completely carefree in my child's world. Even Touna, always so sad, I listened patiently to her moaning, her grumbling, her ranting, knowing not to mention the word, the root of all her pain, the taboo word that she couldn't bear to hear, the word 'Father'.

Sitting on the pavement outside the green front door to Fella's house on the rue Miquel Angelo, I heard her soft voice on a spring evening that was promising a starry sky. She leant on the back of her small wooden chair made by blind orphans at a centre in Tripoli and revealed her secrets.

'Did you know Touna's father was an American from South Carolina? He really was. He worked at the American military base at Mallaha. He was black, a beautiful black man with amber eyes and a smile like an angel. I used to take the bus to go and see him, then his Jeep would take us far from prying eyes to deserted places on the shores of the Mediterranean. We used to lie together on the sand for hours, beneath the stars, trying to pick them out and name them… There's the Plough and look, there, Venus! They were so close to us and there were so many of them we could almost have touched them. We didn't talk much. I knew intuitively he wouldn't stay in Tripoli, he'd go home to his own country, and, thinking I could hold him back, I let him have his own way. It was a blue-black night heavy with the perfume of the Mediterranean and the full moon. We were slightly drunk and happy to be together, like children who can't wait to see each other to get on with their game and forget the rest of the world. There was nothing but us and the completeness of the moment. It was a short night, like those little slices of eternity that sometimes come our way when we manage to throw off the moorings of time and space and bodies. And from that vertiginous moment Touna was born. But by the time I gave birth he was far away, on the other side of the world.

'A black American father and a Jewish mother as white as candle wax! I wasn't the sort of woman you had fun with, you used and then forgot. I was "beautiful Fella, the one and only", the one whose eye and whose smile all the men wanted to catch. To him our escapades were just "a good time", for fun, but to me... he was a fiery boy without a care in the world and I... I was in love.

'As the years passed, the Tripoli Jews gradually forgot about me, then forgave me and eventually started talking to me again. At first I didn't dare go back to the synagogue, but the doorman, Shlomo, dear old Shlomo, your Aunt Hiba's neighbour, came one day, years after Touna was born, when she was twelve, and he said, "It's time you went back to your people." And he took me by the hand, with Touna, and led us to the ancient synagogue in Tripoli, which looks out to sea. In the meantime, American families in Tripoli who knew my story had helped me a lot by offering me cleaning work. As for Touna, Shlomo looked after her, but in secret for fear of losing his standing in the community... We had to wait until the time had come for forgiveness and forgetting. Poor Touna spent her days without me. Shlomo taught her to read Hebrew with the help of stories from the Torah, and he gave her a curiosity for books.

'Touna's never been able to erase her absent father or the dark skin he gave her, and that's what makes her miserable. I tell her to think about Siddena and her situation, so young and no parents! Luckily Siddena works for you. If she'd fallen into the hands of those arrogant Tripolitans... But Touna doesn't hear any of that; she's still so inexperienced. Come to think of it, how is Siddena? Are you good to her? Say hello to her from me and tell her I'm thinking of her.'

Ah yes, Siddena! I remember her face, her features... the very image of a faun, the picture of grace!

It was one of those late afternoons that I spent watching the clouds dance across the sky. In Tripoli these accumulations of condensation stretching across the horizon are a rarity, so I followed them until they almost disappeared, then turned to find new ones and drifted along with them. At that time of day, when the sun was more bearable, I enjoyed watching their changing shapes until the last rays of light died.

Before going up the steps I glanced one last time at the sky to imprint the image on my memory, then headed nonchalantly towards the kitchen in search of some leftovers from lunch. I could hear water, the sound of running water in the basin kept for my Friday ablutions, and I suddenly saw her for the first time, like an apparition, Siddena! No one had warned me that a young black girl was coming to live with us.

There she was, naked. An aura of sadness hung over her, the same sadness I noticed around the black shoeshine boys, the same sadness that emanated from their eyes.

My mother was washing her back with warm water from an old cooking pot. I stood there for a moment, speechless, enraptured. I watched her hunched body. Was she frightened? Did she feel lost or abandoned? Released from the initial spell, my eyes perused her body and settled, fascinated, on her small budding breasts.

My mother noticed me.

'Aren't you ashamed of yourself?' she scolded. 'Go and do something useful. This is Siddena, she's like a sister to you, she's going to live with us to help me with household chores... Hadachinou, don't forget she's your sister, your big sister. When I think how long you've wanted one! She's from Taourgha.'

Taourgha was a village whose population was virtually all blacks descended from slaves bought at Kano; they had followed the slave routes across the Libyan desert, but their journey had ended there. I don't know why... probably to meet the needs of the Tripoli souk.

In the early days Siddena didn't want to speak to me, she avoided me. She knew I was on the prowl when she washed at the basin in the evenings and she didn't seem to like this. One day when she couldn't take my persistence any more, she whisked off to find my mother.

'Auntie, Hadachinou's annoying me! He won't leave me alone. He's always spying on me.'

'He's just a boy,' my mother laughed. 'He won't do you any harm. He's just inquisitive and clingy. Hadachinou –' she turned to me – 'leave Siddena alone and go and play with your dolls.'

The shame of it! I was mortified, and Siddena was the one laughing now as she watched me slip away, only to resume my assault the next day.

From then on she stopped being offended by my presence, occasionally breaking into the beginnings of a mischievous smile; she even ended up enjoying splashing around in the basin, taking her time as she smoothed the sponge over her body with rather suspect application.

The sky was low and dark enough to make anyone depressed.

My mother was with Jamila and my father was at the mosque for evening prayers. I was sitting in the gloom of the small back bedroom, getting lost in the colours on the horizon, when Siddena appeared, walking towards me with a smile and a sideways glance.

'Come, come with me. Don't be frightened,' she said, leading me by the hand. 'Where do you want us to go? Here, in my bedroom? Don't be frightened. Look at me... I'm naked, just the way you like me... It's your turn now. Get undressed. Let's spend some time together, the two of us, OK? We don't have to talk unless you want to tell me anything...'

I only had my *saroual* to take off. I lay down beside her, two children's bodies in all their candour, in the twilight.

Others might have become lovers. We became confidants, arranging to meet whenever the house was empty, to lie side by side again, succumbing to silence or telling each other about our day.

'That first time when you looked at me, I thought you were looking down on me because I was a servant and black, but your mother told me you weren't unkind, just inquisitive. And she said your nickname was Hadachinou. Well, that made me laugh, and after that I quite liked having you hanging around and following me everywhere. I'm fifteen, you know, and I already know all sorts of things. My aunt's a witch and she's told me a whole bunch of stuff.'

I was very surprised to hear that she had trees as ancestors but that her people were also nomads, that their black skin was the mark of the Chosen People of the Light, and they were threads leading from that light. But I was more disturbed when she talked about punishment. Her people had wanted to find the source of the light to achieve immortality, and because of this they were banished from the White Country. They could return to it only after death, after suffering the chastisement of rootlessness and slavery to atone for their sin.

'Being slaves is our punishment,' she said. 'You're my punishment. Serving you and serving other races is the price we must pay till the end of time. By serving, we the People of the Light must learn humility and wash away our shame, and if we succeed in this task, then, when we die, we will end up in the bosom of the Mother Goddess in the White Country.'

Sometimes Siddena called me 'my punishment' to express displeasure or irritation or just to annoy me, but after she'd explained all this it never really made me laugh any more. Particularly because someone else had told me the same thing: 'You're my punishment!' But this person wasn't descended from the Chosen People of the Light. She was my mother.

The heat was so searing and suffocating that even my mother, who was used to the desert winds, lost her customary patience. I hovered around her as if hoping to find some coolness in her shadow. She shoved me aside irritably and cried, 'What a punishment! Oh, Allah, what did I do to you to deserve this? Go and play outside. Leave me alone for a minute... Oh, what a punishment!'

I raced down the stairs, took refuge in the Sidi Mounaïder cemetery and sat there on the sand, leaning up against the marabout's tomb. No one loves me, I'm all alone in the world, I'm never going back home. I'm going to swim all the way to the other side of the sea. There must be a mother who'll love me, and women who'll always be happy to have me around.

Sad as a sinking moon, I eventually fell asleep. Two noisily chirping sparrows whipping up the dust on the neighbouring tomb woke me as the horizon swallowed the eye of the sun.

When I arrived home my mother was in a good mood again, drinking tea with her regulars; she let me put my head on her knees, stroked my hair and pretended to look through it for fleas to justify this sign of tenderness.

'I was properly punished yesterday evening,' one of her friends was saying, 'with my man and my two boys under my feet at home all day. I hate religious holidays! Not only do we have to make them meat dishes for the Feast of the Sacrifice and endless cakes for the Feast of Sugar, but we also have to satisfy their childish whims by day and their fantasies by night. Sometimes I could be driven to murder!'

Nothing shocking about that for this gathering of women, some of whom listened placidly as they carried on lazily chewing their acacia gum, occasionally crushing it and making a loud snapping sound between their teeth, while the others smiled mildly, every now and then their eyes lighting up with a disturbing fire.

'I do what a lot of us do,' the woman went on. 'I spread my legs and let him fuck me. It doesn't last long anyway... thirty seconds, a minute, and there you go! I'm rid of him... What a pain!... Do you remember the woman who chopped off her husband's prick? Well, her husband beat her so much she saw stars in the middle of the day! We all knew, but what could we do about it? Outside the home he was pious and well respected, he went to the mosque every day, but, just like all the rest, he hated women. Do you know what he used to say about his wife? Well, when he was beating the living daylights out of her, he used to say, "Women are all daughters of Satan. Allah made them to test men's hearts. They're the worst trial men have to undergo and men fail thanks to the thousand and one ruses you hellish creatures have!" In the end she flipped and replaced the turmeric in his couscous with rat poison. She watched coldly as he howled with pain, then cut off his parts and chopped him into little pieces she could throw into the disused Turkish latrines behind the old mosque, in among the stagnating shit. Allah forgive me. She even gave chunks of his buttocks to some starving Sloughi. It was a long time before anyone realized, because the other men thought he'd gone off to wash away his sins in Mecca for the umpteenth time. But she must have mentioned it to someone, I don't know who, a traitor, someone who couldn't hold her tongue. You know, men say that we women can't keep a secret... and on that... they're right!'

'But having to carry a secret like that!' the other women retorted as one. 'Just think!'

And to cope with this brief awkward moment, they all gazed into their glasses before gradually picking up the thread of the conversation.

The tea ceremony was the only part of the day when my mother and her friends could live their lives in real time and tell their own stories. At last they could talk about dreams, longings and anxieties all in the same breath, and their bodies were at peace. I sometimes wondered how these women who were all so different were able to spend hours at a time, each talking about her own god, her own people and thoughts, free to be wildly outspoken but without provoking any true conflict. It was because they had no power to preserve and no possessions to watch over. That was for the people on the other side of the wall: the men, the sheikhs, the governors and their hunting dogs! Scheming and calculating, diplomacy and power struggles were their domain. Here with the women, my guardian angels, there were just words, spoken openly and easily, flitting and whirling about, a life force in themselves. Without these moments of trusting abandon, they would have dried up with sorrow. Or imploded as they toiled over their cooking pots.

My own safety valve was Fella.

Fella who could keep my secrets and who listened even when I told her the most outlandish stories: that I was half angel and half human, that I could fly if I wanted to but I restrained myself so as not to attract attention, that I had the gift of clairvoyance, that I could cross time and space without getting lost, that, that... She never interrupted me, indulgently nodding her head like this, up and down, with a tender look in her eye.

I walked through the mirror in my mother's bedroom, I told her. A beautiful round mirror with an old frame of polished wood, a mirror I often stood staring at for a long time in the silence of our empty house. Fella wasn't surprised, and even asked what I'd seen on the other side. So I told her all about it.

'I was just staring into my own eyes when suddenly I found myself on the far side of the mirror. I don't know how it happened, I was only playing with my own stare. Maybe I managed to hypnotize myself?'

'The secret,' said Fella, 'is not wanting it. Then amazing things happen.'

'At first I was walking along a path in a place where it wasn't really day or night, but everything was clear to see. There were trees, rocks, oceans, mountains and deserts made of sand and snow. There was nowhere to go, and every time I thought I'd arrived somewhere I realized I was in the same place, which was everywhere and nowhere. Then I looked at my feet and I didn't have any, and that felt sort of soothing... levitating in that timeless nowhere-land. I was suddenly surrounded by bodies, thousands of bodies, millions of them, just like that.'

'Bodies?' Fella asked, intrigued.

'Women's bodies, Fella, obviously. Masses of women's bodies. Then I could feel my feet again and I was walking over the women's bodies. Bodies that obeyed my every whim. In a flash all the women disappeared except for one, whom I recognized, but at the end of my journey through the mirror I forgot her name and her face. I had this feeling she was the one I'd always been looking for. She was smiling at me from far away, and I chased after her with all my strength, but it was no good. Oh, I was so sad, Fella, and I still am.'

Fella watched me talk, with the slightest hint of a sympathetic smile on her lips. She told me her secrets too, and I promised never to tell them to anyone, except perhaps after she died.

'My body's here but my spirit is in Jerusalem,' she liked to say. 'Not the earthly Jerusalem but the heavenly one, the city of Yahweh, the Nameless One. Sometimes I reach it, and I can be here and there at the same time, but to achieve that I have to read the Torah seven times, and even that doesn't guarantee a result. You have to read the book without making a sound between the words, seeing the letters as the movement of prayer, a trance, without trying to grasp any meaning. That's when they reveal their secrets to the eyes of innocence and surrender.'

Sometimes she was more bitter: 'I'm an angel too, you know, but a disappointed angel. Not so much a fallen angel as one who's been let down. I love the Invisible One, the Nameless One, my Beloved, I abandoned myself to him, his will was my will and his vision was my one wish. But I realized he wasn't aware of my passion or my faithfulness, and he handed out his epiphanies to people made of clay and filth, so I decided to run away, far away.

'But if he doesn't love me I'm sure he must feel very alone, because no man or jinn, and not even an angel, ever surrendered themselves to him the way I did. So it's eternal suffering for me and the hell of loneliness for him. A lonely god without love has nothing but the fear of his chosen people around him, but our god isn't like Siddena's, the god of light. Mine is the god of silence, the god with no name or words. The Torah isn't his word but his silence. We have to look for his word inside ourselves and in the universe. It's an endless quest, and each of us takes a different path to decipher the ineffable god. Some have achieved it, but we can't ask them to tell us about their journey, because when they come to the end of it they vanish into the Invisible, into the Kingdom of Silence. That's why we never stop finding new interpretations of the Book; we are a people of infinite commentaries. I don't know why my ancestors came here to Libya all those centuries ago; perhaps to find the Holy City, a reflection of the invisible Jerusalem.'

I didn't grasp much of what she actually meant, and interjected, 'My mother and her friends all talk at the same time. It's not silence they're looking for; in fact I think they're avoiding it. Their god must be the god of chatter! I don't know what silence is. As far as I can tell, everything talks. Even the Mediterranean has words; you have to listen to the movement of the waves, their outbursts, and then you know it's true.'

'Shush!' Fella said, taking me in her arms. 'Listen. There's nothing, there's just you and me and nothing else. This silence is nothing. When you're on holiday, you're aimless, you don't do anything, you don't want anything, everything flows like a river, effortlessly, spontaneously, like in an empty dream. No worries, no words, no images, nothing, just silence. Shush.'

I didn't like playing with other children. I shared none of their tastes and longings, their shrieks and abrupt changes of heart. I didn't live like a child. As consolation, Fella told me all about women and about herself, sometimes stirring anxieties in me that went unspoken.

'Your mother and the others are angels too,' she said. 'But angels who don't know it. Their punishment is to have forgotten because they deserted God when they realized he was a male god and all he was interested in was his prick and his belly, like all men, his faithful creatures. These women don't know they're being punished and that their punishment is men: yes, the love of men.'

The disappearance of the black American soldier from South Carolina had turned Fella's life and her relationships with men upside down. She'd loathed them ever since.

'Listen to me, little one,' she confided. 'I seduced men to have my revenge, to make them my slaves, to distract them from their lives until they were my loyal worshippers who could even forget their slave status. My body was the bait that they could never actually catch.

'One time at the synagogue there was a man staring at me hungrily. I smiled at him and he followed me to the rue Miquel Angelo. I was alone and I left the front door wide open for him. It was late in the evening. He came in without too much hesitation; I could see him from behind the curtains, but he couldn't make me out because the room was already deep in the colours of night. Then I took him in my arms... When he was asleep I undressed him and perfumed him with aromatic herbs. I burned incense and called on the god of darkness. I cut up his penis and ate it, grilled and seasoned with black pepper and cinnamon; because, unlike pork, a man's flesh doesn't taste of anything. I helped more than one man in this way, spilling blood to return him to virginity... to become a eunuch. They always hid their shame; most have become mystic rabbis possessed by the Unnamed God.'

Tormented by what Fella had confided in me while I was sworn to secrecy, I sneakily quizzed my mother about 'man-eating women'.

She immediately told her friends. 'We're man-eaters!' she joked, and the women were in stitches, particularly Tibra, who would roar with laughter whenever my mother brought up the subject.

Each time Tibra the Berber sat there on our carpet with all her lively enthusiasm, she ignited a pleasant warmth in the pit of my stomach. I don't know how she managed it. I was spellbound, almost salivating if she sat beside me or let me rest my head gently against her thighs, where I could inhale her smell of incense and henna.

How many men had *she* eaten?

And she laughed... how she laughed! Some of the women were in the corridor and others already on the stairs preparing to leave and kissing my mother goodbye. Then I noticed Tibra in the back bedroom setting up a mattress on the floor. So she was going to spend the night at our house!

I went over to her and asked, 'Aunt Tibra, how many men have you eaten?'

'Don't talk nonsense, little man!'

To make her laugh again, I took her in my arms and nibbled her breast.

'You wait,' she cried, pushing me away. 'When you're a grown-up it'll take more than kissing a woman's breasts to win her heart, my little Hadachinou!'

Poor Tibra! She ended up on her own too – all the love-struck men who had asked for her hand had grown jealous; they suspected her of adultery; she could only possibly be a woman of loose morals, knowing so much about love. Not one of them had the strength to stay with her, for fear of being accused of impotence.

'They abandoned me because they couldn't keep up with my body, my desires,' Tibra told my mother that evening. They were sitting on the mattress chatting while I revelled in the complex exhalations emanating from her body and lighting up all of mine. 'They became bitter about their own spinelessness, then they left me for ever, like thieves in the night. The only one who blinded me with love was a Tripolitan, a man who wasn't from the Iftis tribe, an Arab who managed to capture my heart. At first he was gentle, but when I married him he locked me away at home and beat me if he ever caught me looking through the shutters at passers-by in the street. I wasn't even allowed to have my own family over. He hired a man to watch me, a hired man who couldn't resist my charms. I gave him my body and in exchange he closed his eyes and ears, but he ended up bewitched himself, and he went so mad with jealousy and anger and his own powerlessness that he lied to my husband: "Jinns visit her. She summons them using talismans from the black sorceress Hadja Kimya. You said she could see her to ensure her fertility. I could hear them frolicking about the minute you left for the Medina. The black sorceress Hadja Kimya was secretly handing over letters to her from jinns who wanted to couple with her." Drunk with rage, my husband came home unannounced one lunchtime. He grabbed me by the arm and threw me outside, shouting, "Get out, you're possessed, get out! You're the incarnation of evil."

'Even though divorce is taboo in our culture, my family took me back in the hope that this unfortunate experience with an Arab would make me think. Where I come from we avoid contact with Arabs, we don't marry them. Entering into an alliance with them means abandoning our language and traditions, and no longer being part of the free people of Djebel. In the early days, I felt my family had saved me, but I was horrified by their plans to marry me off to an old trader from the Yadder tribe, so I ran away with the first man I found: the colonel in charge of the guardroom. I didn't want to stay in Zouara, my lovely Berber town, any longer because a woman who has tasted the air of Tripoli can never resist the temptation to go back.'

Then she caught sight of me and exclaimed, 'Oh look! Little Hadachinou, there you are! You can listen to this too, then you'll know what it's like to be a woman when you're one of the men... I'm from a different species, a wilder, more ancient creature. Like all women (even if some have forgotten it), I'm directly descended from the Amazons, the warrior goddesses promised to the wind and wedded to the Infinite. They were the hunters and led the tribes when they travelled to new pastures. The men served them. They coupled with the men once a year and killed their male babies, keeping only a few for reproduction. But the people who worshipped a single invisible god arrived across the vast scorching desert. They set up home here and it was a disaster. Our men, who started blindly repeating the words of this invisible god, made them our masters and gave us responsibility for nothing but the *maghzen*, our homes and our beds. And men have paid me dearly for that, very dearly. Now those are the words of a proud woman, neither saint nor whore. Yes, I am an Amazon, a sorceress.'

My mother nodded her head rhythmically, then suddenly said, 'Sorry, Tibra, I'm sure... I swear on the head of Fatima, daughter of the Prophet and daughter of Aïcha, that your guardian angel is doing his job well, or perhaps it's just your destiny to escape men's condemnation and cruelty. There aren't many women like you and Aunt Nafissa and Hadja Kimya. Look what happens to the women who can't give their husbands children! How many women dare go out alone and look men in the eye? Do you know what one local man did to his wife when she went to hospital to see a doctor without his permission? She was having trouble breathing, poor thing, and was often terribly out of breath. Every time she complained about it to her husband, he brushed her aside with a "stop being such a pain! I've got better things to be doing... Go on, piss off, filthy thing!" And when he found out that she'd dared go to the doctor, he sliced off her nose and rejected her, saying, "Now you've got no nostrils you'll be able to breathe perfectly well." You see, Tibra, you know about all that. You tell me about the Amazons, and it's good to hear, but there aren't women like you and Aunt Nafissa and Hadja Kimya on every street corner in Tripoli... Amazons, you say! Slaves, yes!'

To be honest, when I heard Tibra use the word Amazon I didn't immediately grasp what it meant. But when she called herself a sorceress, that instantly made me think of Kimya, the black sorceress Hadja Kimya, whom everyone respected and feared, not because she had made the pilgrimage to Mecca, but because she had the power to communicate with jinns and inhabitants of the Invisible.

Like Siddena, Hadja Kimya was originally from the village of Taourgha, descended from slaves. Her father had given her in service to a major tradesman, a pious well-known man, who abused the girl by night. Young Kimya was constantly afraid and never stopped crying. She mentioned it to her mistress, who then beat her out of pique and jealousy. The Muslims taught their slaves to pray to Allah, and Kimya prayed to Allah constantly, but it did no good. One day she kept the master's grandson entertained by playing with a doll. She noticed that the doll had no genitals. She went to the kitchen and cut her finger, and sprinkled blood over the doll's groin. All of a sudden, an invisible strength took possession of her, making her pronounce strange words against her will.

Eventually she regained control. She turned to the mistress of the house. 'This evening your husband will go to hell,' she said calmly.

Out of fear or mistrust, no one wanted to talk to her after that. They avoided her. Except for Nafissa, who stayed at Kimya's house on her visits to Tripoli. Aunt Nafissa introduced Hadja Kimya to her friends and, mildly amused, they went to her for consultations. They were sceptical at first, but over time became loyal and grateful customers, and this turned them into sworn enemies of sheikhs and doctors.

Hadja Kimya mixed with other women only when Aunt Nafissa was there. They liked being together, whispering in chorus and appreciatively sipping from glasses of *boukha*, an alcohol made from figs whose smell alone made me recoil in disgust.

When towards the end of summer the scorching *ghibli* wind arrived to ripen the dates, with it appeared a black man who brought jars of date palm wine for the women. They gave me some of this delicious liquor before it was fermented. Hadja Kimya had so much of it that her eyes swivelled in their sockets and gazed aimlessly off into infinity. Aunt Nafissa sat silently, listening to the sorceress's words.

'I am Kimya, the woman from the end of time that will soon come for all men. I am the chosen one of the world of darkness, of its secret lights and sacred babblings. I was born before time, born of a sugary flower the colour of silk. My people live on the other side of the light. I am the goddess with no tablets of laws or commandments. My spirit is everywhere and nowhere: I am the invisible visible, the interior exterior, the absent presence, the sleeper awake, the beautiful and the ugly, the merciless and the compassionate. I am the bosom of the world, the abyss of roses, the fragrance of every new dawn. I am the bird of shadows, the tree of floods, the only star of the eastern lands. I am the night. Before loving I hate and when I love I burn. I become the other person: the enigma. The strange, the stranger, the queen of cycles, the dream of pollen, the fall of angels...

'I can see you're laughing, Nafissa, and I'll allow it because it's you. I know why you're laughing... Because I tell you this: in my vagina lies the secret of the universe and from my breath whole worlds are born and wonders, dreams and winds. If you only knew, Nafissa!

'You think I'm inspired by the goddess of the night. But it's her own voice you hear when I speak; she and I are the same and each other. You don't have to believe what I'm telling you, Nafissa, but magic and clairvoyance are serious matters, and if you weren't my friend something terrible would have happened to you by now, because my companions, the jinns, would not have tolerated being defied... You're still laughing at least I can make you laugh. Go on, go on, laugh. One day you'll realize I'm telling the truth. I come from the belly of the night, the ring of light, the goddess of worlds.

'I order the jinns to protect and heal. And to descend like scourges, to annihilate. By night I welcome my ancestors, the black sorcerers, into my dreams. I pray they will deign to come and give me advice. They initiate me so that I can help the dying to leave this earth without getting trapped between myriad worlds. I guide them across the realm of death to be resurrected in the empire of night, in the bosom of our goddess of the eternal darkness.'

Hadja Kimya made men impotent and cured sterile women, but she was no more accepted by the Tripoli community than other black people. Despite appearances, marriages between blacks, Berbers, Arabs and other children of Tripoli were still rare. The locals called the blacks 'shoeshine boys' or *abids*, slaves. I saw them lined up one beside the other, leaning against the walls of the great Banca di Roma. The oldest among them coolly chewed on Tuscan cigars, while the youngest sat quietly and waited for customers, their eyes immeasurably empty.

My 'sister' Siddena was also pained by the fact that she was different and that she had been snatched from her people as a tiny child. Her mother worked for a friend of Aunt Nafissa's and she could only visit her on religious holidays. She never even knew her father; when she was born in Taourgha he was no longer among the living. He apparently died the day of a great drinking bout. People said he'd shown a lack of respect for one of his fellow drinkers by spilling wine on his *chechia* hat, so his master – intoxicated with rage as well as wine

– allegedly decapitated him with a large knife normally used for cutting off sheep's heads. His body was thrown to stray Sloughis at dawn.

No one ever tried to shed any light on the exact circumstances of his death; he was an *abid*, a meaningless slave. Siddena and her mother never knew the true facts and had to settle for the official version: 'His lifeless body was found after a battle against the colonizers.' Her husband's elevation from *abid* to *moujahid* – freedom fighter – far from displeased his wife, though.

When I took Siddena with me to Aunt Nafissa on one of her all too rare visits to Tripoli and Siddena bemoaned her fate as a poor little black girl despised and forgotten by her own people, Aunt Nafissa told us the story of the little fly. At first we laughed, but Aunt Nafissa warned us, 'You'd do better to listen to my stories instead of laughing at them, because they carry in them memories of our countries, particularly the country of women.' Then she began:

I'm a fly, a tiny little fly. I was born on a pile of shit, and I've loved eating it ever since.

The day I came into the world of Homo sapiens, *a torrid sun was devastating the land. The wadis were empty, water scarce, the sea dried up; many died. Our tribe, the Medina flies, was first in line to inspect the putrefying bodies. Flies from the outskirts of the city patiently waited their turn, and sometimes ended up with nothing because* Homo sapiens *came and buried their dead kinsfolk before we'd finished our feasting.*

My father liked nostrils best. He would sneak inside them with my older brothers and sisters, and spend ages in there. Sometimes they would have their siesta inside, and they even defecated there. I myself preferred the eyes – a delicacy, my mother used to say; she often came with me to watch out for approaching Homo sapiens.

That year, the drought was ravaging the land for our benefit, but there was more: much to our delight, Homo sapiens *went to war against each other. Our tribe had a great deal to do. Those were feast days. There were so many bodies everywhere that we shared our meals perfectly peacefully with jackals, foxes and Sloughis.*

In normal drought years, we made do with the bodies of newborns or poor wretches strewn about on the ground with their bellies split open. But those wild bewitched lands carried on nurturing generations of men, women and slaves... that's what my grandmother used to tell me before I went to sleep. She would come to see me when I'd eaten my fill and my belly was nicely distended, and she would teach me about the world.

My mother never came to my bedside and told me stories to settle me in the evenings before I went to sleep. Did she know any? I can't be sure. What about my grandmother? I would spend whole afternoons with her and she wouldn't say a single word, communicating her affection with tender looks or filling me with sweetmeats that she baked just for me. That was how the time passed as we sat side by side on the terrace or lay gazing at the sky.

When I was at her house in Arc de Badawi, my grandmother was never in a hurry to get on with her household chores. She barely spoke to her husband, limiting exchanges to the indispensable. They each had their own bedroom, and my grandfather stayed shut away in his all day, smoking and grinding his teeth. Their house – the bedrooms, the landing, even the furniture – seemed to me like something from a dream, from another world, a different history.

If I'm honest, I was a bit bored at my grandmother's house. I loved and respected her but I couldn't settle there; I didn't feel I was allowed to play. I had nothing much to do, and so one day I was absent-mindedly kicking a stray piece of wood around on the terrace when I carelessly let it fall on to the roof of a car. The driver braked, jumped out of the car and barked, 'Where are the police? Someone throw this filthy vandal in the lock-up! The son of a whore!'

My grandmother glided silently into the kitchen, took a big saucepan, went calmly down the steps, using the wall for support, and walked out of the door. She went up to the ranting young man and, still perfectly calm, unleashed her temper on him to the point of almost breaking the saucepan.

'You worthless son of a dog, son of a mule!' she shrieked. 'Do you know what the whore says? You've still got shit between your buttocks and you think you're a grown man, you good-for-nothing, you bastard...' She carried on punctuating her words with thumps of the saucepan: 'You don't know anything about war and hardship, you never had a taste of Mussolini or had to starve, you young...'

No one dared intervene – not the neighbours, who knew what she was like, or the police, who took the young man to hospital and gave him a talking-to, insisting it was just a minor incident but that there was definitely never any justification for calling an old woman a whore.

I couldn't have dreamed of more spirited protection, but I was still surprised and a little uneasy to discover violence like that under such a peaceful exterior.

That evening on the terrace she said, 'You always want me to tell you stories, but I only know stories about the war and suffering. You'll learn them soon enough from books… or by yourself.'

I didn't want to know about my country's past so much as about my family's, to know its origins. When I asked my mother where I came from, she replied, 'From the dustbin next to Sidi Mounaïder cemetery! Someone left you there and ran away.' But when she burst out laughing I knew she was teasing me. Then I would try satisfying my curiosity by asking the mirror, but the only answer it gave me was a hazy sketch of a constantly evolving portrait.

'Who am I?' I asked the sheikh at school.

'You are an Arab and a Muslim,' he replied proudly, with a smile.

I quizzed the mirror: 'Arab, Muslim, but what does that mean?'

It gave no reply.

The following day, still puzzled, I went back to the sheikh with more questions: 'I'm an Arab and a Muslim, but what does that mean exactly?'

'Arabic is the language chosen by Allah to speak to men, and being a Muslim means adopting that language.'

When I went to the mosque with my father for the Friday prayer ritual, I trotted out endless verses with the other boys, but I was troubled by conflicting voices inside me. I found all that kneeling before the Great One absurd, when he was so merciful that he let those who didn't follow him burn in hell and made their flesh recover so he could be sure to perpetuate their torture for all eternity. Let their screaming and their pain be eternal! Yes, that bit I understood and remembered! I didn't like this particular 'invisible one', but I didn't dare say so because I would have been seen as a monster.

It started bothering me reciting this language without understanding what I was saying. A frozen, mummified language. Even if I succeeded in hiding my feelings from the sheikh by playing up the fact that I was always sleepy, I wondered what the mirror would make of the state I was in. The mirror never lied: I became invisible and my image became more diffuse as my hate grew. I was a faceless body; in my dreams I no longer even saw my body. I existed without being. At this point I believed that, without Allah's language, I wasn't in his world.

Mummy, Mummy, my longed-for refuge.

'Mummy! I tell you about all my dreams but you never tell me anything, not about yourself or your marriage or where I'm from or who my ancestors are!'

'Go on, go and play outside or go and look in your mirror... Out of my sight!'

Fella told me I didn't disappear in the mirror but I just wasn't there, drifting absent-mindedly as usual, or blinded by the sun without realizing it. Her explanation failed to convince me, but the fact that she paid attention to my questions appeased me for a while.

Nafissa, though, was the only one who could shed any light on things.

'My little Hadachinou,' she said, 'even if we can find the names of our own ancestors and work out whether they're descended from Arabs or Berbers or the nations that believed they conquered Tripoli, no one truly knows where they come from. As for the sheikhs, they're just parrots droning on saying the same thing since forever... Do you know what Allah means? Allah means astonishment. And if you astonish yourself, what do you say? You say "Ah", don't you? Allah just means that: it means "Ah!" It's that moment when an apparition or an event captivates us, or when we're simply amazed by little aspects of everyday life. That's when Allah reveals himself. It's men and their power struggles who have formalized something that was originally a state of pure wonder and recognition; they gave it a fearsome name and face, even a beard. And they're dragging the whole world along with them into the blinding abyss because, instead of questioning this enigmatic beauty, they flood the world with a tide of words... and deaths.

'Look into my eyes, my little Hadachinou. What do you see? You can see yourself in my pupils and me in yours, ad infinitum. Do you understand? You come in ⁓h my eyes, you're in my blood, adding to my ₁g through my kingdom, my gardens, my labyrinths, then you come through my mouth, you emerge, soft kisses... Another person's eyes are your origins and your kingdom. But these other people can't see *you* if they're blinded by their search for an illusion, for the Invisible One.'

It was the light itself, real and palpable, that took me in its embrace that night: my mother and I were lying resting, totally relaxed and trusting, on the sunny terrace when all of a sudden the day sucked me up into its hand and put me back down into my bed, eyes wide open, already bathed in the first dancing rays of sunlight. As usual, I ran to tell her my dream and share the rapturous moment with her. My mother was busying herself with baskets of tomatoes and large bowls; she put a bowl at my feet. What could I say? I started energetically crushing the juicy flesh. Pleased with myself and my gallantry, I then ran to Fella's house, a valiant messenger sent to invite her to tea that afternoon, but mostly to talk to her for a while.

The only person there was her daughter, Touna, sitting stiffly on her chair as she so often did, with her hands crossed in her lap and an absent expression on her face. So I carried on with my usual circuit.

I didn't find my grandmother at home, and my far from talkative grandfather shook his head to indicate that he didn't know where she was, so I sat down thoughtfully in the middle of the wasteland opposite their house. My lovely grandmother! I could picture her baking *ghraibas*, little biscuits made of flour, sugar and butter, treats I gulped down greedily three or four at a time. She sometimes spent days preparing them. It was her way of taking revenge on the years of hardship, making up for lost time, eating cakes and sweets to silence an ancestral famine. Her cooking talents were well known, and when she produced *haraïmi*, a sort of fish soup, a good many Tripolitans hung about hoping for an invitation from my grandfather. He would grant them this favour if they bought the traditional leather sandals he made. So plenty of people had more than one spare pair of sandals! My grandmother worked away at her oven in silence, not even realizing she was passing on to me the secrets of her cooking.

From there I went to the cemetery, head lowered, lost, adrift in faceless daydreams, tripping on uneven paving stones and bumping into the occasional lamp post insidiously put in my way. I spoke to the marabout, listened to the birds and headed off to enjoy the company of the Mediterranean. Its presence gave me a sense of calm, as if underground rivers deep inside me stopped churning.

My own private itinerary through the labyrinth of Tripoli: the Sidi Mounaïder cemetery, the marabout's tomb, the wastelands on the outskirts and the port on the Mediterranean.

Looking out to sea, I remembered what Hadja Kimya had said: 'Hadachinou, keep yourself busy doing simple things that delight you. Give yourself a goal. The soul of life is the little things, the minor events no one notices… That's where life is, the pleasure of being alive, otherwise there's just this vast blueness casting its shadow over us. Go on, keep yourself busy, do something, and then you might find yourself one day.'

At home I was showered with criticisms: 'So, did you go to Fella's? No? Honestly! But what have you been doing all this time? Where have you *been*? You're useless! If I sent you to sea you'd find it had evaporated! Did you at least tell Touna we're expecting to see her mother this afternoon?'

When my mother had finished her diatribe, she didn't even wait for me to explain myself before chivvying me out of her women's gathering, while the others continued with their chatter, unconcerned. Now exiled, I took refuge on the roof of the back bedroom, where the twilight sky gradually started to twinkle shyly.

And, as often happens when the night decides to divulge its secrets, the darkness was vast, like a confession of love. The stars looked on calmly as they busily wove the sky's face. They were there in their groups, jostling for position as if wanting to console me with an initial burst of chaotic movement, for once forgetting their place in the heavenly hierarchy so that I could touch them with my hand. My bare feet dangled over the roof of the small, cold, dark back bedroom. The air swirled gently in the whitish light of the full moon, a moon suffused with soft melancholy since the separation of worlds. Its despairing eyes stared at me in distress; my presence reminded it, yet again, of its deep wound, the wound of being separated from its nurturing mother, the sun.

I jiggled my feet as if wanting to touch the walls of marabout Sidi Mounaïder's cemetery several dozen metres away. I could feel the heat from lanterns hanging here and there, and thought I could make out the marabout's helpless whispering, his devastated voice as he lulled to his bosom the dead who had been buried that day, before they undertook the other journey, without bodies, without words, without baggage, escorted by the princess of darkness, the night, that fretwork of light.

Pictures came together, spooled past, waking dreams. In the distance I could make out the muted gasp of the sea and the voice of the sorceress Hadja Kimya coming to me from other floods and divulging fragments of her book: 'Take care of your soul as the wind does, have fun on your own as a butterfly does and live within yourself as a mountain does. The others are just mirrors. They exist only if you let them inside you. Only the horizon is endlessly reborn from its fall. The world is a land of strident sound and blindness, life is the home of silence and sight. In this world and in a dream, apart from the unforeseen, there is only darkness. Along the way there is no meaning; all meaning is an illusion, a lie. The earth and the sky, little silences both of them, are the only things that talk. You are just a way of seeing things, so open the windows to your eyes. You need only your eyes to fly away, your eyelashes are your wings and the look in your eyes is your face, inhabiting your own face, flying away, reaching that other country, changing your dreams, finding other shores…'

It was timeless, listening to Hadja Kimya as she initiated me into her world and her words.

Through the closed shutters I can make out the flickering glow of the candles my mother likes to light as night falls.

I open the door like a traveller with no provisions after a day of wandering and I'm gripped by an unexpected feeling of warmth: Aunt Fatima's penetrating voice and a shrill laugh from Houda, her Houda, reverberating from the top of the stairs.

'Ah, here's Hadachinou! Where's this little man been, then? He looks tired. Come and sit next to me. I'll tell you a story.'

Seven girls inside a…

Peirene

Contemporary European Literature. Thought provoking, well designed, short.

'Two-hour books to be devoured in a single sitting: literary cinema for those fatigued by film.' TLS

Online Bookshop

Subscriptions

Literary Salons

Reading Guides

Publisher's Blog

www.peirenepress.com

Follow us on twitter and Facebook @PeirenePress
Peirene Press is building a community of passionate readers.
We love to hear your comments and ideas.
Please email the publisher at: meike.ziervogel@peirenepress.com

Subscribe

Peirene Press publishes series of world-class contemporary novellas. An annual subscription consists of three books chosen from across the world connected by a single theme.

The books will be sent out in December (in time for Christmas), May and September. Any title in the series already in print when you order will be posted immediately.

The perfect way for book lovers to collect all the Peirene titles.

'A class act.' GUARDIAN

'An invaluable contribution to our cultural life.'
ANDREW MOTION

£35   1 Year Subscription (3 books, free p&p)

£65   2 Year Subscription (6 books, free p&p)

£90   3 Year Subscription (9 books, free p&p)

Peirene Press, 17 Cheverton Road, London N19 3BB
T 020 7686 1941
E subscriptions@peirenepress.com

www.peirenepress.com/shop
with secure online ordering facility

Peirene's Series

FEMALE VOICE: INNER REALITIES

NO 1
Beside the Sea by Véronique Olmi
Translated from the French by Adriana Hunter
'It should be read.' GUARDIAN

NO 2
Stone in a Landslide by Maria Barbal
Translated from the Catalan by Laura McGloughlin and Paul Mitchell
'Understated power.' FINANCIAL TIMES

NO 3
Portrait of the Mother as a Young Woman
by Friedrich Christian Delius
Translated from the German by Jamie Bulloch
'A small masterpiece.' TLS

....
MALE DILEMMA: QUESTS FOR INTIMACY

NO 4
Next World Novella by Matthias Politycki
Translated from the German by Anthea Bell
'Inventive and deeply affecting.' INDEPENDENT

NO 5
Tomorrow Pamplona by Jan van Mersbergen
Translated from the Dutch by Laura Watkinson
'An impressive work.' DAILY MAIL

NO 6
Maybe This Time by Alois Hotschnig
Translated from the Austrian German by Tess Lewis
'Weird, creepy and ambiguous.' GUARDIAN

COMING-OF-AGE: TOWARDS IDENTITY

NO 13
The Dead Lake by Hamid Ismailov
Translated from the Russian by Andrew Bromfield
'Immense poetic power.' GUARDIAN

NO 14
The Blue Room by Hanne Ørstavik
Translated from the Norwegian by Deborah Dawkin
'One of the most important writers in Nordic contemporary literature.' MORGENBLADET

NO 15
Under the Tripoli Sky by Kamal Ben Hameda
Translated from the French by Adriana Hunter
'Straight out of a Vittorio de Sica film.' CULTURES SUD

. . . .
NEW IN 2015
CHANCE ENCOUNTERS

NO 16
White Hunger by Aki Ollikainen
Translated from the Finnish by Emily Jeremiah and Fleur Jeremiah
'A novella that feels like a huge, great novel.'
SATAKUNNAN KANSA

NO 17
Reader To Hire by Raymond Jean
Translated from the French by Adriana Hunter
'A book that will make you want to read more books.'
COSMOPOLITAN

NO 18
The Looking-Glass Sisters by Gøhril Gabrielsen
Translated from the Norwegian by John Irons
'Raw and dark and wonderfully different from anything else.' DAG OG TID

Peirene Press is proud to support the Maya Centre.

The Maya Centre

counselling for women

The Maya Centre provides free psychodynamic counselling and group psychotherapy for women on low incomes in London. The counselling is offered in many different languages, including Arabic, Turkish and Portuguese. The centre also undertakes educational work on women's mental health issues.

By buying this book you help the Maya Centre to continue their pioneering services.
Peirene Press will donate 50p from the sale of this book to the Maya Centre.

www.mayacentre.org.uk